Torrie & the Snake-Prince

Text by
K.V. Johansen

Illustrations by
Christine Delezenne

 annick press
toronto + new york + vancouver

Annick Press Ltd.

We acknowledge the support of the Canada Council for the Arts, the Ontario Arts Council,
and the Government of Canada through the Book Publishing Industry Development Program
(BPIDP) for our publishing activities.

Edited by Pam Robertson
Copy edited and proofread by Melissa Edwards
Cover and interior design by Irvin Cheung/iCheung Design
Cover and interior illustrations by Christine Delezenne

The text was typeset in Perpetua and Egyptienne

Cataloguing in Publication

Johansen, K. V. (Krista V.), 1968-

Torrie and the snake-prince / text by K.V. Johansen ; illustrations by Christine Delezenne.

(The Torrie quests)
For ages 9-11.
ISBN-13: 978-1-55451-070-2 (bound)
ISBN-13: 978-1-55451-069-6 (pbk.)
ISBN-10: 1-55451-070-8 (bound)
ISBN-10: 1-55451-069-4 (pbk.)

I. Delezenne, Christine   II. Title.   III. Series: Johansen, K. V. (Krista V.),
1968-   Torrie quests.

PS8569.O267T676 2007   jC813'.54   C2006-906464-4

Published in the U.S.A. by
Annick Press (U.S.) Ltd.

Distributed in Canada by
Firefly Books Ltd.
66 Leek Crescent
Richmond Hill, ON
L4B 1H1

Distributed in the U.S.A. by
Firefly Books (U.S.) Inc.
P.O. Box 1338
Ellicott Station
Buffalo, NY 14205

Printed and bound in Canada
Visit our website at **www.annickpress.com**

to Tristanne
holdwine ond rædbora

Glossary of People, Places, Things, and Old Things

About Old Things and the Wild Forest

Old Things are ancient, magical beings; in the time that this story takes place, humans still believed in them, though they didn't see them very often. Some Old Things say they have been in the world as long as humans have, or longer...but they like to tell stories, so who knows? There are many different kinds of Old Things. Most can't be seen by humans unless they want to be seen, but others, like goblins, have to rely on being sneaky. Some look a lot like humans; most don't. Many of them have magical powers, and they're always most powerful when they're in their own place, the place they belong to, the way Torrie belongs to the Wild Forest.

The Wild Forest is a vast, strange, uncharted forest north of Erythroth and the Mountains, and west of the sea. Torrie is the oldest Old Thing of the Wild Forest, but there are many other Old Things living there. The only humans in the Forest tend to be either lost or having adventures, although a few solitary witches, hermits, and wanderers (who aren't lost) do live there.

Some kinds of Old Things

Dryads are tree-spirits, usually appearing as beautiful women. Naiads are water-spirits, but there aren't any in this story. Still, it's a useful word to know.

The Fair Folk of the Mounds are sometimes called fairies by humans. They seem like tall, beautiful humans, with very powerful magic. Even other Old Things don't see them very often. Like most Old Things, they are very long-lived. Humans and Fair Folk sometimes marry, but life can be very difficult for their children, who don't fit well into either world.

Goblins, in the north of the world where this story happens, are gray and hairy and have red eyes. They don't like the sunlight. They do like to fight, and steal, and smash things up for the fun of it. They're not very bright. Although they are a type of Old Thing, most of them don't live any longer than humans (a few do, though), and none of them can be invisible to human eyes.

Griffins are a type of magical creature, and whether they're animals or Old Things is something sorcerers like to argue about. The truth is, some of them are Old Things who are very wise and live for centuries, but others are more like animals who can think and speak like humans. They have the head and wings of an eagle, an eagle's legs for their forefeet, and the body, hind legs, and tail of a lion. The males are smaller and more brightly colored than the females. They lay eggs in high aeries.

About the People (and Animals, and Old Things)

Torrie is the oldest Old Thing of the Wild Forest. He looks like a small furry person with big pointy ears and yellow eyes. You might say that human-watching is his hobby——he often goes on adventures with young humans, just to see what will happen.

Lord Abastor (Abastor Sultanzada): a sorcerer.

Sir Acer: the captain of the Twenty-Seven Royal Knights of Morroway, and the King's Champion.

Ash: Wren's dapple-gray mountain pony.

The birch dryad: lives in a grove of birch trees and doesn't like goblins much. Who does?

Bobbin: a goblin, who is very annoyed at Lord Abastor.

King Boiga: king of High Morroway and father of Liasis.

Queen Demansia: King Boiga's wife, stepmother of Liasis.

Sir Eglantine: a red-haired young knight, a good friend of Prince Liasis. Sir Rufous is her brother.

Farancia: a maidservant in Morroway Castle. She usually wakes Liasis up in the morning.

Fleabane: a goblin.

Crown Prince Liasis: one of the heroes. Bad things happen to him. If they didn't, there wouldn't be a story, would there?

Prince Notechis: uncle of Liasis.

Rookfeather (Rookfeather Khanum Sultana): a mysterious wandering minstrel. She's a good friend of Queen Demansia's. (If you look very carefully, you can find a mention of her in *Torrie and the Firebird*.)

Sir Rufous: another one of the Twenty-Seven Knights, and a friend of Liasis's.

Sir Salix: another one of the Knights, and the wife of Sir Acer.

Snip and Snag: the former goblin chiefs.

Swallow: Sir Eglantine's warhorse.

Thimble: a goblin with no sense of direction. Bobbin's younger brother.

Toby: a yellow dog who lives in Hampstead-Above-The-Falls.

Torrie: see *Some kinds of Old Things*.

Wren: a hero. She does something about the bad things happening to Liasis. Actually, when the story starts, she's a pedlar, which is someone who wanders around selling things. Wren is beginning to think she should find something more exciting to do with her life when, luckily, she finds Torrie.

About the Places

Callipepla: a country which lies far to the south of Erythroth. It's a sultanate, which means it's ruled by a sultan, who seems to be a relative of Rookfeather's.

Erythroth: the kingdom south of the Wild Forest. It's separated from the Forest by a chain of high mountains. Wren is from Erythroth.

The Great Musquash: a big swamp in the Wild Forest.

Hampstead-Above-The-Falls: a village in High Morroway, famous for its double waterfall.

High Morroway: a small kingdom in the mountains between the Wild Forest and Erythroth, famous for its cheeses.

Hollidon: the capital city of Erythroth, on the east coast of the country. Wren grew up in an orphanage in Hollidon.

King's Town: where the famous Royal Cheese Fair is held every fall. It lies below Morroway Castle and is the only big town in High Morroway.

Morroway Castle: the royal castle in High Morroway.

The Mountains: a range of high mountains that runs west from the sea and eventually curves north, like a wall around the Wild Forest. If they have a name, Torrie hasn't mentioned it yet.

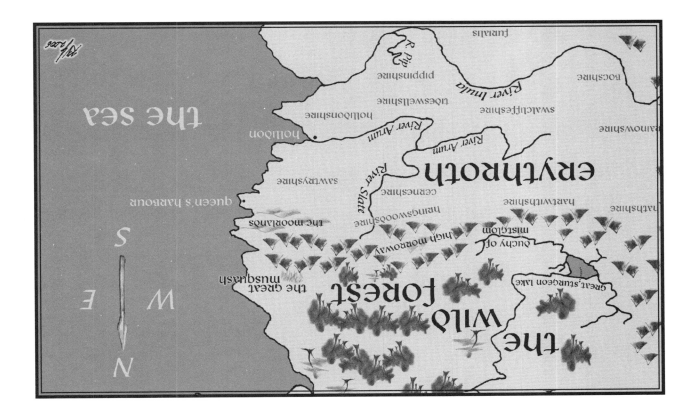

CHAPTER ONE

In which a prince goes missing

Long before I ever went dragon-hunting or sailed the South Seas, I went on a quest in my own land, the Wild Forest. But the adventure actually began in High Morroway, a small kingdom almost lost in the towering, snow-capped mountains that lie between the Forest and Erythroth.

It all started on a cool spring night, with the frogs singing in the ponds. Liasis, the Crown Prince of High Morroway, had stayed up long past his bedtime, reading about the goblin wars by the light of a single candle. When a sudden sharp breeze whirled in the window of his tower room and snuffed the candle out, he yawned. Lighting it again seemed like too much work so very late at night, so he set the book on the table by his bed and pulled the blanket up over his ears.

Outside his door, something creaked. It was the noise that usually woke him in the morning—the floorboards creaking as Farancia, the maid, brought him a pitcher of hot wash-water.

Liasis rolled over to look towards the door. It was open, and the faint starlight showed a dark figure.

Prince Liasis might have been half asleep, but he knew he wasn't dreaming. He stretched a hand out from under the bedclothes to the table by the bed. His fingers groped over the smooth leather of the book's binding and the cold metal of the candlestick. They touched the odd, lumpy packet that was the present he meant to give his stepmother, Queen Demansia, for her birthday in the morning.

The gift was a fish made from scraps of tin and copper wired together. When you held it up in the sunlight, hanging on a couple of fine threads, it seemed to twist and shimmer like a real fish leaping up the waterfalls in the spring. Liasis hoped it would please his stepmother. She still didn't seem very happy in High Morroway, and, although of course she would never take his mother's place, he felt very protective of her, as if she were a timid young aunt.

Liasis had bought the fish from a pedlar girl he met on the road when he was out riding two days before. She had made it herself, and he thought there was a bit of the girl's own spirit in the shimmering fish—free and wild and full of joy. Demansia needed to feel that happiness.

But the tin fish wasn't what Liasis wanted. His fingers found the hilt of his dagger and closed around it. He always kept the dagger by his bed, not because he was afraid of enemies, but because it had been a gift from his own mother on his ninth birthday, his last birthday before she died, four years ago. He slid the blade out of its sheath.

"Who's there?" Liasis demanded.

The dark figure said nothing, but it took a step closer. As Liasis swept the blankets back and sat up, knocking everything clattering off the table, whoever it was flung something towards him.

A net. He saw the glitter of its strands as it settled over him, covering him from head to toe even as he tried to beat it off. It was like the nets used for fishing in the mountain lakes, but far, far finer, as though it had been knotted out of spider-silk. There were odd, glittering things caught in it. Fish scales? Liasis flailed his arms frantically and yelled for help, but his room was at the top of the empty east tower. He'd liked the privacy, the feeling that the whole tower was his own place. Now it meant that no one could hear him.

The strands burned cold where they touched his skin, rather like the feeling you get when you grab frosty metal in the winter. And then they tightened, as if they were shrinking around him, pulling his arms to his sides, binding his legs together, constricting his chest so that he felt he could hardly breathe.

"Help!" he gasped, much more faintly now. "*Somebody!*"

Nobody came. After one abrupt jerk, as if his attacker had almost moved to help him, the person just stood there, watching.

Prince Liasis fell to the floor, thrashing and twitching. The floor felt…different. He felt…different. He made a dash for the door, fast as an arrow on his stomach, but the dark figure swooped down and grabbed him around the neck, flipping him into—a sack. A rough, dark, musty-tasting sack. The sack began to bounce, as though the person carrying it was walking quickly, and then to jounce as the person ran down the spiraling staircase.

Liasis couldn't remember what had happened to his dagger. He tried to grope around for it, but he couldn't feel his arms. He was paralyzed, he thought, but no, he could thrash about violently, so he couldn't be paralyzed. He couldn't feel his legs. He could feel—*sack*, all over his body, rasping on his smooth scales.

Scales.

Liasis opened his mouth to scream, and all that came out was a faint, hissing breath. He flailed frantically from side to side, as though he could somehow smash his way out and back into his own body, but all that happened was that the person gave the bag an angry shake, stunning him into stillness.

Liasis heard a door open, the one that let out from a lower floor of the tower on to the castle wall. He felt the person carrying him lean out through one of the crenels, the gaps in the battlements from which archers would shoot.

Someone whistled. There was an answering whistle from below.

"Here," said a voice. "Remember, you promised he wouldn't be hurt. You promised nobody would be hurt." Liasis couldn't recognize the voice; he couldn't even tell if it was a man's or a woman's. It was strangely distorted, distant and rumbling.

"I did," said another voice. "And I keep my word. Tell me, has the potion started to work?"

"If it hadn't, I wouldn't be doing this. I always keep *my* promises, too. Did you bring the rest of the mixture?"

"There's a jar, corked and sealed with wax, down in the grass at the foot of the tree where we met. You can fetch it from there in the morning. There should be enough for half a cupful once a day for two weeks, and that will be all that's needed."

"Can I trust you?"

"It's a bit late to ask that now." The second voice laughed, hollow and booming. Liasis was almost certain it belonged to a man. He, if it was a he, was echoed by a chorus of hooting, screeching, cackling laughter, until that second voice said, "Silence!"

There was silence, broken only by the first voice saying, very faintly, "I'm sorry, Your Highness."

And then Liasis was falling, plummeting towards the ground.

The castle was a collection of towers and narrow little yards all jammed together, with a high wall that had always looked to the prince like a strap tying up the bundle of towers. It was perched on top of a rocky crag in the heart of the mountainous kingdom. It had no moat, no water to catch him and save him. He was going to die when he hit the stones…

The sack stopped falling with a jerk as someone caught it out of the air. Hooves rapped on stones as the man urged his mount away. Even these ordinary sounds were oddly altered by the change to his body, seeming further away and deeper than they should be. The prince could hear something else, too, like the pattering of many soft feet.

In his sack, Liasis bumped against the horse's side. He felt horribly, horribly sick. He didn't think snakes could throw up. He hoped they couldn't, at least.

IN MORROWAY CASTLE THE NEXT MORNING, the maid who came to wake Prince Liasis wasn't too surprised to find him gone. It was a beautiful day, the sort of day when everyone, prince or peasant, would want to be outdoors. Farancia picked up his nightshirt, which was dropped untidily on the floor, and the blankets, which were all over the place. Then she saw the things from his table, scattered across the room.

Her foot touched the dagger, lying where it had fallen, half under the bed.

Anyone would have known for certain that something was wrong, then. The prince always wore that dagger on his belt.

Farancia took the dagger and the tin fish and went down all the long stairs to the solar, which was a bright, sunny room where the royal family gathered. King Boiga was there, eating fried trout and scrambled eggs, with Queen Demansia, who was nibbling a piece of toast and looking nervous. But the queen always seemed to look nervous. It might have had something to do with the fact that most of the servants in the castle thought she wasn't good enough for their king. After all, she hadn't even been born in High Morroway.

Quietly sipping a cup of tea in a corner was a stranger, a tall, brown-skinned woman with piercing green eyes above a narrow, beaky nose, in which she wore a ruby. She had gold rings in both ears and two black feathers tucked into her long, untidy black hair. The woman took her name from those: Rookfeather. She was a minstrel, who tramped the roads of the world carrying songs and stories and news from one kingdom to another.

Prince Notechis, the king's brother, was there too, carefully checking over his fishing-flies, made of bits of feather and fur tightly bound to sharp hooks. He sucked a pricked finger and said, continuing an argument that had begun before the maid came in, "But it just isn't safe for the queen to go out riding in the forest right now, Boiga, you know that. You know how the people feel about her. Remember how someone threw an egg at her last time she rode through the town?"

"Just boyish high spirits," growled the king. "And when the knights catch the person who did it, they'll get the spanking a boy deserves, even if they turn out to be a granny of a hundred and three."

Prince Notechis rolled his eyes and gave the little, black-haired queen an apologetic smile. "It isn't her fault, but she is a foreigner, and your people don't trust her. They think you should have married someone from High Morroway. There are people who—I hate to have to say this, brother—but there are a few people who suspect Demansia of wanting to get rid of poor Liasis, so that when she has a baby herself it will be heir to the crown."

"No, never!" the little queen cried at that, dropping her toast. "I couldn't love Liasis more if he were my very own!"

Prince Notechis patted her hand in a calming way. "I know, I know. I just think Boiga needs to know what a few dangerous elements are saying, that's all. And that's why it isn't safe for you to go out riding in the forest."

"Nonsense," King Boiga said, slurping his tea. "If Demansia wants to go out riding, Demansia shall go out riding. It's her birthday, for goodness' sake! I'll accompany her myself. How could anyone want to harm her?" And he took his wife's tiny hand and kissed it.

King Boiga was a big, blond, rough-looking bear of a man, but whenever he looked at Demansia his eyes crinkled up into a smile.

It was then that Farancia decided to speak. She curtsied, and said, "Excuse me, Your Graces, but I think something might have happened to Prince Liasis. I found this on the floor of his room, but I can't find him." And she set the dagger on the breakfast table. She put the fish beside it. "And this. He got it from some pedlar he met on the road. It was supposed to be a gift for the queen."

"So he went out without his dagger," the king said. "There's no reason to fuss about a little thing like that."

"He never leaves it behind, Your Grace. And the room was a terrible mess."

"Boys are messy," said the king, waving a hand.

"But Liasis is always very considerate and tidy," said Demansia.

"It looked to me," said the maid grimly, "as though he was fighting someone up there."

"Nonsense!" said King Boiga. But he surged to his feet and swept out, heading for the stairs to the prince's tower. The queen, wide-eyed and anxious, hurried after him.

Rookfeather the minstrel picked up the fish and watched it twirl and glimmer in the light. She looked very thoughtful.

Afterwards, people forgot what had actually happened and said, *The prince was missing and the maid found a strange foreign ornament belonging to the queen on the floor of his room.* Meaning, the queen must have been there, and dropped her ornament while struggling with the prince. Humans just aren't very logical, sometimes.

THEY SEARCHED THE CASTLE, every tower and every cellar. They searched the stables, and the kennels, and the mews where the falcons were kept. They searched the kitchen-gardens where vegetables and herbs were grown, and the tiny rose-garden.

Liasis's horse was still in the stable, and his dogs were still in the kennel. When the housekeeper searched through his wardrobe, she found that all his clothes were still there.

Wherever the prince was, he must be naked.

The minstrel went quietly up to the highest room of the east tower and looked around it herself. She looked at the table, and the bed, and the floor, sometimes with her eyes half-closed. She picked a wisp of something like spider-silk off the bed, and a strand of blond hair from the pillow. Then she picked up two greenish-brown scales from the floor. All these she folded up in a piece of silk torn from her wide, tattered sleeve. Then she went outside and walked around the castle walls. She paced back and forth along the eastern side of the castle for some time, staring at the ground.

Then Rookfeather went inside and talked privately to the queen, until Prince Notechis came with four of the Royal Knights to arrest the minstrel. She was the only suspicious foreign person in the castle to arrest, and people felt someone had to be arrested.

The queen cried, and when that didn't work, she went pale, with a spot of red in each cheek.

"Rookfeather Khanum Sultana is a dear friend of my uncle," she began to say, but Prince Notechis raised his hand warningly.

"Don't!" he said. "What are people going to think? Everyone knows your uncle is a Court Enchanter to the Sultan of Callipepla."

"Yes," said the queen. "Exactly. He would not be a good person to annoy."

"He might be the sort of person who could make a prince vanish by sorcery," Prince Notechis said, lowering his voice. "Do you want people saying that? People saying it's some Callipeplan plot, and that you're a part of it?"

Of course, it didn't matter how quietly he said it. No sooner were the words spoken then some of the servants, who had crowded in after the prince and the knights, were repeating them.

"But you can't!" Queen Demansia said. "You mustn't! Rookfeather is the only one who can…"

"It's all right, Your Grace," said the minstrel, and she patted the queen's shoulder in a comforting way. "I'll be fine. They'll release me in a few days, when reason prevails, and if it doesn't…" she gave Demansia a quick flash of a smile, "…*you* know I'll be fine."

Rookfeather waved the four knights out the door ahead of her as if they were a royal escort, not a prisoner's guard, and Prince Notechis actually gave her a somewhat embarrassed half-bow as she followed, because he knew what Khanum Sultana meant, even if the guards didn't. "*Hazretleri*," he murmured politely, hoping he had the correct Callipeplan word for "Your Highness." He'd had no idea the queen's ragged friend was someone of such high rank.

WHISPERS ABOUT ENCHANTERS and sorcery and foreign plots swept through the castle, passed between servants and soldiers, clerks and courtiers. No one could remember who first said, "The queen, his stepmother—she must know something about it, too!" But not long after the minstrel was locked up, half the castle was crying, "Question the queen!" and then, "Arrest the queen!"

"How dare you!" King Boiga roared at the first person who was foolish enough to say it in his hearing, "Anyone who repeats such a thing will be thrown into the dungeons—and I'll do the throwing in person!"

"I love Liasis!" the queen cried. "I'd never harm him. How could anyone think such a thing? And if he's been kidnapped by magic, Rookfeather is the only one who can find him and bring him back! I don't care if you arrest me, but let her go!" And she burst into tears.

"Calm down, everybody, let's all just calm down," said Prince Notechis, pulling anxiously at his beard. "There's no need for all this. Nobody is going to arrest the queen; of course not. But," he added, "it might be best, for Her Grace's safety, if she stayed in her own rooms, with guards at the door."

"I'd rather be locked up with Rookfeather, if the people of High Morroway hate me so much that they'll believe such horrible things about me!" the queen cried.

"Don't be foolish, darling," the king said. "No one in *my* kingdom would dare believe you could do anything so wicked, even if you are a lowlander."

Queen Demansia's face went very pale, and then very red. "Don't be an idiot, Boiga!" she said. "I never thought you could be such a—a High Morrowaian snob. If you really loved your son you'd send Rookfeather out to look for him!"

"Oh, don't!" said Prince Notechis. "You're both upset and saying things you don't mean." The king's brother looked from Boiga to Demansia and back again. Both the king and queen were glowering, their lips thin, their faces flushed. "Probably it would be best if you went to your rooms to calm down," he suggested. "I'll organize the search for Prince Liasis. I've already summoned the Twenty-Seven Royal Knights."

The king and the queen went off to separate apartments in the castle without even looking at one another. Prince Notechis sighed. Although he looked like a skinnier version of his roaring bear of a big brother, the king, all Notechis really wanted was a quiet life, with lots of time to go fishing. He said so, whenever anyone asked him why he didn't ride off seeking adventure in foreign lands, the way younger princes were supposed to in those days.

In the distance, two separate doors slammed.

After that it was very quiet in Castle Morroway.

CHAPTER TWO

In which I meet Wren, and a goblin

I had decided, that spring, to visit High Morroway. Although my home is the Wild Forest, occasionally I like to go off wandering, when my feet start to itch, and then I usually fall into an adventure of some sort or other. I did hear rumors about the mysterious disappearance of Prince Liasis, but most of the stories blamed it all on the queen and her friend, the Callipeplan minstrel, and that sounded like Politics to me, rather than any interesting sort of quest. Politics is a human vice that I prefer to avoid.

One day, though, in the middle of May, more than half a month after the prince had vanished, I met a girl traveling through the mountains. The wind carried the scent of wild plum-blossom and the setting sun washed everything in rosy light as she came along the path, leading a sure-footed mountain pony heavily laden with baskets and bundles. The girl limped, using a stout staff to help herself along, but she was walking briskly, and it seemed to me that she was quite used to the limp and didn't really notice it at all. I had been stretched out on the branch of a pine tree, dozing, but I sat up as the girl approached. She looked to me as though she was probably about fourteen years old or so, all big hands and feet, like a puppy not quite grown. Her hair was brown, short, and curly; her skin was pale, and she had cloud-gray eyes. She was wearing patched gray wool trousers and a sky-blue shirt with a baggy brown tunic belted over it, sturdy boots (one of which looked rather strange), and a dark brown cloak, also patched. Into her floppy-brimmed, reddish felt hat she had stuck an assortment of feathers. She passed beneath me, whistling a tune, the dapple-gray pony following close behind. I watched her continue along the stony track. It was quite a ways to the next village; probably she meant to camp out on the mountainside tonight, I thought.

"Fair Jessamine's taken the long, long road…" she now sang cheerfully. "…over the hills and away…"

I climbed down from the tree and trotted after her.

Introducing myself to a new human can sometimes be a bit tricky. Although these days most of us try to avoid humans, when this story happened, Old Things and humans had a lot more to do with one another. They knew we might help them out once in a while, so they sometimes left us little gifts, like a bowl of milk or a loaf of bread. Despite that, we didn't let them see us very often. You never knew how a human might react to someone like me suddenly appearing, and humans also knew that iron is a charm against us — we can't stand the touch of iron.

It gives me a rash, and it can do much, much worse things to some of us, although goblins don't seem to mind iron at all—which is a pity, because if there's one sort of Old Thing you'd want a charm against, it's a goblin. This girl had a knife in her belt, and her sturdy staff had an iron spike on it. I wanted to be sure I was right about her before making myself visible. I didn't want to be mistaken for a goblin.

Not that anyone who had ever seen a real goblin would mistake me for one. I'm Torrie, and I'm the oldest of the Old Things of the Wild Forest. I'm about three feet tall. I have long fingers and toes, big pointy ears (very good for hearing with), and sharp little fangs, like a fox or a cat. Some people say my nose is too large, but since it's my nose, it must be just the right size for me. My eyes are golden-yellow and my fur is rusty red-brown and rather shaggy.

All we Old Things are magical, in one way or another. Almost all of us can talk to animals as easily as we can to humans, and almost all of us can only be seen by humans when we choose to be, which is very useful, as you can imagine. Actually, invisibility is one power goblins don't have, so they've become very sly and sneaking instead.

The girl did not go much farther before making camp. She left the path where a shallow stream burbled across it and unloaded the pony in a sheltered dell, with the pines and the water making music on either side.

"I'm a rover," the girl sang, starting a new song as she unloaded the pony and rubbed him down, being careful to clean out his hooves. "I'm a rambler, and I'll never go home..."

She gave the pony a handful of grain and only started gathering wood for her fire once he was contentedly grazing. I approved of the way she looked after the pony first, although it meant that dusk had fallen by the time she had her fire crackling and could start her supper. I watched as she mixed up a stiff dough of flour and oatmeal, setting the bannock cake to bake on a rock, and her kettle to boil beside it. My stomach rumbled at the smell. While the bannock baked she sat down close to the fire and began working with tin-cutters and pliers.

Every now and then she would hold the thing she was making up into the firelight to get a better look at it, and I would lean down from the boulder where I was perched, and take a good look too.

But I wasn't the only creature watching her. There was her pony, of course, but there was also another. As long as he only watched, I was willing to pretend I hadn't seen him. But I kept him in the corner of my eye.

The thing the girl was making seemed to be a collection of odd scraps of copper and tin, held together with fine wires and thread, with some bits of glass bead and a few blue jay feathers. As I watched, she plucked a white dove's feather from the band of her hat and wove it into the web of wires. And then, when she turned it a little, it sparked to life in the firelight and became a glorious, shimmering sky-dragon, spiraling up into the air. And then it was only a pretty, sparkling ornament again. A human might hang it over a baby's cradle or in a window to catch the sun. But when this human girl leaned over with her pliers to clip and snip and twist, and her body cast a shadow over it, I could see a warm, amber glow running along the wires, if I squinted my eyes just so. *Magic*.

It didn't seem to me that she even knew what she was doing, but I could see that there was a little echo of herself going into it, a free, wild, joy in life that would make anyone who looked at the sky-dragon ornament feel a little of that same joy and freedom. It was a strong, good magic.

"Who is she?" I asked the pony.

He lifted his head and looked at me thoughtfully, still munching, ears pricked.

"You're not a goblin, are you?" he asked. "I don't speak to goblins."

"Do I look like a goblin?" I said, watching out of the corner of my eye, where something skinny and gray, with knobbly knees and elbows and shaggy hair on his head and shoulders, was still crouched among the rocks. *That*, as you can probably tell from my description, *was* a goblin. He wore a moth-eaten fur kilt that might have been skunk-skin, but it was so old and grubby it was hard to tell. If it had been skunk, it had lost all its scent long ago. Which was really too bad, because skunk would have been better than unwashed goblin.

"Or do I smell like a goblin?" I asked, to give the pony a hint.

"No, not really. But you can't be too careful, these days. The trails aren't as safe as they used to be."

"That's true enough," I agreed, with a stern look over at the rocks.

Some horses hate goblins, and will attack them on sight. Some are terrified and will bolt. I didn't know whether I should warn the pony or not. He might be a bolter. Probably it was better not to risk it. Goblins are great cowards, and I didn't think that a lone goblin was going to attack the girl with me there.

"I'm Torrie," I said. "Of the Wild Forest. And you are?"

"Ash," the pony said, and shivered a fly off his shoulder. He ripped up another bite of grass and chewed it thoughtfully. "She's Wren the Pedlar."

"What's she making?"

"Supper," said Ash. "Bannock. I've been very good today. Maybe she'll give me a bite."

"No," I said patiently. That's the problem with talking to animals. Food is often the only thing on their minds. Not unlike goblins.

"I meant," I explained to Ash, "what's she making out of all the bits of metal?"

Ash looked at the girl. You might think he seemed a bit dim-witted, but that wasn't true. Humans are always twiddling with something, and usually it's not anything very interesting to horses.

"Oh," he said. "That's just one of her fancies. She mostly makes them in the winter, when we're not traveling."

"What's a fancy?"

Ash nodded his head at Wren's busy hands. "That is. She uses scraps of metal and ribbons and feathers and shells, and she turns them into fish and birds and horses. I like the horses, especially. Look, that's one on my harness. She made it just for me. Pretty, isn't it? She used my hair."

I looked, and on the breast-strap of the pack-saddle, stacked neatly out of the way with the baskets, was fastened a little glimmering bit of metal. It was mostly tin and red ribbons and a few twists of horsehair and didn't look like much of anything, but when the breeze stirred the horsehair, for a moment I saw a little running horse, flickering silver and fiery in the light of the flames. It was a charm to keep a horse strong and safe and healthy, and neither of them realized it.

"You said she was a pedlar. Does she sell a lot of those fancies?" I asked.

"Oh yes," said Ash proudly. "Mostly she sells pins and ribbons and penknives and buttons and stuff like that, of course, but people seem to really like the fancies. Up here, the villagers say if you hang one of Wren's fancies over a baby's cradle, it'll sleep all night. They say the fancies give children good dreams. Sick people feel a little better, if one's hung over the bed. They even hang them in the barns, because they say the cows give more milk. It's just—what's that human word? Superstition, of course. But if they sell well, that means more oats for me next winter, so let the humans believe they're magic if they want. Wren says if they make people happy, that's good enough, because she likes making them."

"Maybe they *are* magic," I suggested, to see what the pony would say.

"How could they be?" he asked. "It's not like she's a sorcerer. I've seen enchanters in Hollidon, going to the queen's court. They wear velvet robes and gold rings and ride Callipeplan horses. With *pedigrees*," he added, with a mixture of envy and respect.

Ash had some very odd ideas about what made someone a sorcerer, but I didn't set him straight. I was looking at Wren and realizing that she was what my itchy, adventure-seeking feet had been heading towards.

And, as you probably suspect, I was so interested in what Ash was telling me that I stopped watching the goblin.

Wren set aside her sky-dragon fancy and flipped the bannock onto a tin plate with the blade of her knife.

"If you want to follow, then follow you can, But don't ask me to stay with a shoe-making man!" she sang cheerfully.

That was when the goblin flung himself off the stones where he had been crouching and snatched the piping-hot bannock off the plate, cramming the whole thing into his snaggle-toothed mouth.

"Get away!" I hissed, and I threw a stone at him. This was in the days before I got my dragon-hunting spear and I didn't have any weapons at all, while the goblin had a rusty iron knife. It just isn't right: an Old Thing, even a goblin, with an iron or steel weapon.

The goblin yelped as my stone hit his leg, but he didn't drop the bannock. He dodged around the fire, heading for Wren's bundles. I don't know if he meant to hide behind them or grab something out of them, but I picked up another stone.

Wren leapt up, balancing mostly on her left foot with her staff held crosswise in her hands. It wasn't just a mountain-climbing staff, I realized. It was also a quarterstaff, meant for fighting. With one quick flick she swept the goblin's feet out from under him, and with a twist and a *thwack* she struck him in the ribs as he was falling and knocked him flying. He gave a muffled yelp and vanished into the darkness.

Ash flicked his tail and pulled up another mouthful of grass. "You didn't need to worry, Torrie. Wren's good at goblins." And he rolled up his lip in a horsy snicker at me.

I was quite impressed, and I didn't mind admitting it. "She's not much like a finicky little wren," I observed. "More like an eagle."

"So much for bannock," Wren muttered. "That was the last of the oatmeal." She used the blade of her knife to lift the steaming kettle off the fire and threw a handful of mint leaves into the boiling water. That was when I got a good look at her right foot, which was all twisted and crooked. She couldn't set it properly against the ground, except for the thick sole of her oddly-shaped, high-heeled right boot.

Then she looked straight at me and frowned, squinting a little, as if she was trying to see something that wasn't quite there. Which I should have been, as far as she was concerned. I did explain that most of us OldThings can't be seen by humans unless we want to be, didn't I? Sorcerers can sometimes see us even when we're invisible, most often as just a bit of mist or a shimmer like heat over stones. I once met a human who wasn't a sorcerer at all but who could see me all the time—although I found out later her grandmother wasn't entirely human, so that explained it. But a pedlar wasn't the same as a trained sorcerer. This girl must have a very strong talent for magic, I decided. It was odd no one had realized it and found her a master to apprentice with.

"Hello," she said then, and tilted her head, so she did look a little like a wren. "Are you…there is someone there, isn't there?"

While I was hesitating, not quite sure whether to show myself properly or not, she reached into one of her packs and pulled out a large cheese, carving off a chunk with her knife. "Want some supper? I've got some dried apple slices, too."

I do like High Morrowaian cheese.

"I know where there's a duck's nest," I said, letting her see me properly. "She'll never miss two or three eggs."

"An Old Thing!" she said, and she grinned with delight. "I've always wanted to meet one of you. I'll unpack my frying pan."

Later, as we ate our supper and drank mint tea, talking of this and that and getting to know one another, I asked Wren about her foot. I wasn't being rude, and she knew I wasn't. I was simply curious.

"What happened to your foot? Were you injured in a battle or something?"

Wren waggled her boot and laughed. "A battle? No. They call it a club foot," she explained. "I was born this way. It never grew properly."

I scratched my ear thoughtfully. "So why are you a pedlar? Is it a family tradition? Wouldn't it be easier, with a bad foot, to be something that doesn't involve climbing up and down mountains?"

Wren snorted. "Easier, yes."

"But?" I prompted.

"But why do what's easy?" She grinned. "That'd be so boring, wouldn't it?" Then she was serious again, turning the cup we were sharing around and around in her hands, her eyes fixed on it while her mind was elsewhere.

"I want to be free," Wren said slowly. "Like the birds. Like the wind. All my life, that's what I've wanted." She looked up at me and passed the cup back. "I was abandoned at an orphanage, down in the city of Hollidon in Erythroth. Left at the gate in a basket one summer night."

"Not a family tradition, then," I said, sipping the tea.

She grinned wryly. "How do you know? Maybe all my ancestors were foundlings, left at orphanage gates."

"I meant being a pedlar."

"I know what you meant. No, I'm not following in anyone's footsteps, so far as I know. Sometimes I think I'd like to know. I wonder about my family, who they were, what they did. Why they didn't want me." Wren looked at her foot. "I hope it wasn't because of *that*. I hope—what I mean is, it's nicer to think my mother was just some poor woman, who couldn't look after a baby and did the best she could, making sure I was someplace I would be cared for. Or that maybe she died—not that I want to think she died, but you know what I mean—if she had died and maybe there was just an old grandmother, someone who couldn't look after a baby...I don't want to think I had parents who got rid of me because I wasn't perfect."

"If they did, you were better off without them."

Wren made a face. "That's true. Anyway, the orphanage wasn't bad. The people were kind, but it was very—organized. Everybody had to get up at the same time and wash at the same time and eat and sleep at the same time. It was like living in a cage. You couldn't just get out when you wanted. And when you get older, they try to find apprenticeships for you. They decided that because I was always trying to make my own shoe more comfortable for my crooked foot, I'd make a good cobbler—a shoemaker. So they apprenticed me to a cobbler, four years ago."

"You didn't like cobbling?"

Wren shrugged. "It might have been all right, I suppose. It's making things. I like making things." She took the empty cup from me and I poured her some more tea. "And the cobbler was a nice man. But sitting inside at the bench in the shop all day, every day, year after year after year, cutting leather, stitching, hammering, never able to just stop and wander someplace else under the open sky... Never able to see new things, never being able to do anything that mattered—I know shoes matter, try going without them—but..."

"But I do go without them," I said, wiggling a bare foot in the air.

Wren poked me in the ribs. "You know what I mean. It was just going to be another cage. I hate staying inside all day. So I ran away. Like the prince."

"You mean Liasis?" I asked. "The one even the cows and the barn-cats are talking about?"

"Are they?"

"The humans talk about it so much even their animals are interested."

Wren nodded. I didn't have to explain that I could understand the animals, because in those days, as I've said, humans still told a lot of stories about us Old Things and, what's more, they believed them. Just a couple of centuries later, they had already started to forget, and now... Anyway, Wren wasn't surprised. She asked, "So what do the cows and the barn-cats say?"

"Probably the same thing the humans you talk to are saying."

"Ah," said Wren. "So you know most people are saying that his stepmother, the queen, worked some evil sorcery to get rid of him. There's supposed to have been a strange minstrel from Callipepla at the castle, Rookfeather, a friend of the queen's. She was arrested, I heard. But quite recently Queen Demansia made the king let her go. Some people are saying King Boiga was bespelled by the queen, and that it's up to Prince Notechis, his brother, to save the kingdom. And I heard there was a band of goblins roaming around King's Town, and some people are saying they stole the prince."

"I hadn't heard that," I said.

"Oh yes. Lugged him away in a sack for one of their feasts."

Wren grinned, enjoying herself. Carrying news—and rumors, which are often more colorful and exciting—is part of what people expect from pedlars and other tramping folk. "The king sent out the Twenty-Seven Royal Knights of Morroway to follow the goblin trail, and..." she lowered her voice like a proper storyteller, drawing me in, "…*they never came back.* Not the last I heard, anyway," she added.

"But you don't believe any of those rumors?" I asked.

Wren shook her head. "All the different versions of the story say Liasis simply vanished from his bedchamber one night, and I can't imagine goblins getting into the castle. And why on earth would Callipepla want to cause trouble in High Morroway? It's so far away from here. I think he ran away. After all, being a crown prince must mean living your life in a sort of cage, too. All royal duties, day after day, year after year, no freedom to wander."

"Not everyone wants to wander," I pointed out. The story puzzled me. Goblins wouldn't steal a prince to eat, not a half-grown one twice their size. Goblins don't eat humans all that often, anyway. They're too cowardly, and humans usually fight back. But, if the prince had run away, as Wren suggested, then what had happened to the knights?

"How did you end up a pedlar?" I asked, getting back to her original tale. "What did you have to peddle?"

Wren laughed. "Not a lot. I had a few pennies saved of my own. I bought a big basket and as many cheap ribbons and pins as I could afford, and I set off to be a pedlar. And people did buy things." Wren laughed again, her eyes bright in the firelight.

"I think they felt sorry for me. But I lived on black bread and turnips, because that was the cheapest food I could get, and I saved my money and I bought a few better things. And I could always see the mountains, off on the northern horizon. I wanted to get to those mountains. When winter came I couldn't go tramping the roads any more, so I lived in the stable of an inn in return for mucking out the stalls. I started making my fancies out of scraps other people were throwing away, and I sold them in Hollidon market. The next spring I bought Ash to carry my baskets, even though that took all my money and meant black bread and turnips again. And I did get to the mountains. It's not that far from Erythroth up into High Morroway, really. I've been coming back every year since." She waved a hand around. "You can feel *free*, up here. Although I'd like to…" Her voice trailed off.

"Like to what?"

Wren shook her head. "I don't know. Something different. Something *more*. This spring——I don't know. I guess I'm just feeling restless, somehow. The mountains aren't enough."

"I know just what you mean. What you need," I said wisely, "is an adventure."

Wren laughed at me. "Will we meet the prince, disguised as a wandering fiddler? You look like the sort of Old Thing who makes adventures happen."

"I don't make things happen. I just like to hang around when they do."

"So you do think something's going to happen?"

"Who knows? Maybe that depends on you."

But I was quite sure that something would happen. Wren's own story proved she was the kind of person who didn't wait around for someone else to work things out for her. *She* was the one who made things happen.

I didn't mention magic to Wren at that time. Power is a tricky thing. Sometimes it's better to grow into it, than to have it all thrust on you at once before you're ready.

CHAPTER THREE

In which Wren accepts a quest

"Buttons and beads!" Wren sang. "Ribbons and bells! Penknives and perfumes! What do you lack? Wren the Pedlar's here!"

On a rainy evening, a few days after I joined Wren and Ash on their travels, we tramped into Hampstead-Above-The-Falls. The little village was famous for its two waterfalls, which would have been quite pretty on a sunny day, but there was nothing about Hampstead to suggest it was the sort of place where a girl's life might change forever, a new path she'd never imagined opening up right before her feet, waiting for her to step on to it. But for Wren, that's just what Hampstead was. Of course, you hardly ever do recognize a moment like that, when it comes. You just step, and it's only later, looking back, that you can say, that was the moment when I changed my world. Or, sometimes, that was the moment I could have…and I didn't.

As we splashed and squelched our way up the muddy lane that wound through the houses and barns of Hampstead-Above-The-Falls that fateful day, I found myself wondering if the entire village had vanished, like Crown Prince Liasis and the Twenty-Seven Royal Knights. There wasn't a human in sight.

"Strange," Wren remarked, noticing it too. "Surely it's too late in the evening for everyone to be off in the fields. And anyway, it's too wet." She repeated her call, more loudly. "Buttons and beads! Ribbons and fancies! Pedlar, pedlar— what do you lack?"

Not a single pair of eyes even peeked out a window at us.

"Hey!" I called to a skinny yellow dog who was sitting in the doorway of a barn, watching the rain with a look of boredom on her pointy face. "Where are all the humans?"

She looked up to where I was perched on Ash's back amid the baskets, invisible to any humans except Wren, not that there were any humans to notice. Or not to notice, I mean. The dog sniffed heavily for a few moments, the fur on the back of her neck and in a line down her spine standing on end.

"Are you sure you're not a goblin?" she asked suspiciously.

"You don't look like one, but…"

"Do I smell like a goblin?" I demanded.

"A little, yes."

"Well, I'm not. I'm just damp, that's all. Everyone's fur smells when they're damp. Even yours. You smell like an old fish, but you don't hear me accusing you of being a herring. This is Wren the Pedlar, and Ash, and I'm Torrie."

"*The* Torrie?" the dog asked. "Of the Wild Forest?"

"Yes," I said modestly. "That's me."

"Hm," the dog said, and her fur flattened down again.

"I'm Toby."

"So where are they all?" I repeated. "Has something happened?"

"Everyone went to the inn to see the minstrel." Toby looked thoughtful. "*She* smelled very strange, too," the dog added.

"Like a goblin?"

"Nooo…" the dog said. "Not exactly like a goblin. But strange. A bit like you. A bit like a goblin. Like a wild thing."

"What are you doing, getting the story of its life?" Wren asked impatiently, leaning on her staff.

"Just finding out where everyone is," I explained.

"So where are they?"

"She says they're at the inn."

"Then why are we standing in the rain?" Ash asked, and tugged his rope out of Wren's hand, breaking into a trot again.

"Then why are we standing in the rain?" Wren asked, and ran after Ash and me. Her steps were rather uneven, but that never stopped her from running.

THE INN IN HAMPSTEAD-ABOVE-THE-FALLS was really just another farmhouse, but the farmer and his wife rented a few rooms to those rare travelers who came to the village, and served home-brewed ale to their neighbors in their big front parlor.

Most High Morrowaian houses were the same. They had steep roofs and a balcony under the eaves, with a veranda along the front, and window-shutters painted with mountain flowers and birds and hearts, just like their doors. And they always had a wide, deep fireplace, with a bake-oven in the wall beside it for bread and pies. As we drew near the inn I could smell bread, of course, and a fine herby, oniony smell that was probably a chicken pie, and of course there would be three or four kinds of cheese to have with the bread, since this was High Morroway.... My stomach rumbled so loudly that Wren heard and laughed at me.

"Being invisible isn't going to do you any good if you make noises like that," she said, and she ran up onto the veranda and leaned over the lower half of the door—High Morrowaian front doors were usually divided in two, and except in the winter, the top half was open all day. "Hello the house!" she called inside. "Wren the Pedlar's here!"

In a moment a boy had whisked Ash off to the stable, promising him a bran mash and a good brushing, and Wren, with her bundles and baskets slung over her shoulders, was wiping her boots on the innkeeper's doormat and looking over the crowded front room. Toby the dog had been right: all the village was here. They were crowded up at the one long table, and packed in close together on the benches that ran around three sides of the room, while the children clustered in a corner, giggling and whispering. On the fourth side, opposite the front door and beside the one to the kitchen, was the big fireplace. Sitting on a stool by the fire, her brass-strung harp on her lap, was the minstrel.

She was tall, and her long, tangled hair was coal-black, streaked with gray, but she did not look very old for a human, not more than forty or so. Her skin was brown and her eyes were as green as leaves. Her clothing was all silk, layers of bright reds and blues and greens, fluttering with ribbons and tattered hems. There were gold rings in her ears, a ruby glowed in the side of her nose, and she wore two long black feathers tucked into her hair. You recognize her, of course. I did, and Wren did, though we had never seen her before. She was the minstrel who had been in the castle the night Prince Liasis disappeared. Rookfeather, Queen Demansia's friend.

The people of Hampstead recognized her too. Their expressions reminded me of the way Toby had sniffed at me.

Rookfeather obviously knew the villagers were suspicious, but she merely looked amused, as if she knew that, no matter how much they disliked her, there wasn't a thing they could do to harm her.

However, they were happy enough to see Wren.

"Welcome, pedlar, welcome," the innkeeper said, and his wife found her a seat. Someone else took her sopping hat and cloak, and in a moment a big piece of chicken pie was set in front of her, with a stack of bread and cheese beside it, and buttermilk to drink.

I crawled under the table and peered out between all the farmers' boots at the minstrel. She took a deep drink from her tankard of ale and smiled at the crowd, as though they were making her as welcome as they had made Wren.

Wren passed me down a large slab of warm bread-and-butter and a chunk of my favorite cheese, the slightly brownish, nutty-flavored one.

"I can see you don't want to believe me," the minstrel said, continuing whatever she had been saying when we came in. "But that's the truth. Queen Demansia has asked me to find a hero to rescue her stepson, who was kidnapped by goblins." She drew her fingers over the strings of her harp, first a flutter of notes, and then the slow, ringing beginning of a solemn tune.

"But probably you have no heroes here," Rookfeather continued, "and no room in your inn, either, for the likes of me..." and she smiled in an amused, superior way, as though it couldn't possibly matter what they thought of her, "...so I'll give you a song before I leave."

We Old Things are very hard to lie to, and there was truth in the minstrel's voice, but true words or not, I wasn't certain I blamed the villagers for being so mistrustful. I didn't think the minstrel had anything to do with the prince disappearing, but there *was* something odd about her. Not quite a smell, and definitely not goblins...

Hah, I thought. *Magic.* Not sorcery; messing around with spells and rituals, which is how those humans with a talent for magic give a shape to their power, but old, deep, in-the-blood-and-bones magic. This minstrel didn't need to work a spell to influence the world around her. All it needed was her will, her wanting something to happen, for it to become more likely things would go the way she wished them to.

Which is the sort of thing I do, although I prefer not to have to.

The chords the minstrel struck from her harp silenced even the giggling children, and she began to sing. She had a voice that was meant for singing—not too high, not too sweet, but rich as honey. Her song was a slow, mournful ballad about a princess trapped in a tower, and how a prince set out to save her, but grew tired and lost hope of ever finding her and gave up his quest. So the princess turned into a bird and flew away alone when she realized no one would ever rescue her. By the time the minstrel was halfway through I was ready to dash out of the inn and rescue all the sad, lost people I could find. Of course, I often do that sort of thing anyway.

That's what the magic Rookfeather was putting into the song was supposed to do: inspire people to think about riding to the rescue. It wouldn't force anyone to do anything they didn't want to do. That would be terribly evil, about the worst thing a sorcerer or any other magical creature could ever do. But there's nothing wrong with giving people a nudge towards the right path. They still don't have to take it, but you can hope.

Some of the villagers looked thoughtful, and their faces seemed more kindly as they watched the minstrel. I couldn't see Wren's face, but her foot was tapping in a considering way.

And suddenly the song was over and the minstrel rose, with her hair and her tattered sleeves and hems and all the bright ribbons that trailed from her clothes swirling around her. She swept the room a bow and then bowed again to the two innkeepers and their son, who had come in from the stable for the last part of the song. For a moment, the gesture transformed the homely, comfortable inn to an elegant royal hall, all dark polished ebony and gilded pillars, and her ragged silk seemed a shimmering robe, with half-seen jewels glinting in its folds.

"Thank you for the meal," she said to them. "And consider your queen's plea. Heroes aren't born wearing gilded armor and brandishing a sword. I know. I've met a few. You'd be surprised how often you can sit down to supper with one without ever realizing it."

The innkeeper's wife seemed embarrassed by how coldly they had all treated the minstrel. "It's pouring rain, Mistress Rookfeather," she said. "You can't leave yet. Stay the night and sing for us again."

But Rookfeather, kneeling on the floor to tuck her harp into an oiled leather bag, shook her head. "Your queen has asked me to seek in all the villages of High Morroway for someone to save Liasis. There seem to be no heroes here, so I must be on my way."

She was mocking them again, and didn't care if they knew it. Then the minstrel flashed a sudden smile across the room towards the table, but she was still crouching with one knee on the floor, and it wasn't the faces above the table she smiled at. It was at me, down there among the boots. No human in that inn but Wren should have been able to see me.

It was a very knowing smile. "Heroes aren't born," she said. "They happen."

That was exactly what I believed: a hero is a hero because of what they *choose* to do. But even though she was looking at me, she aimed those words straight at Wren.

And I thought I caught a flash of an eyetooth that was just a little too sharp to be human. Rookfeather laughed, silently. She swung a thick, black cloak over her shoulders, and then, with three quick strides, she was gone from the inn.

Wren's feet twitched as if she had almost leapt up to follow. Even though it had seemed to me since I met her that Wren was heading into an adventure, I wasn't sure I liked the way the minstrel was assuming the girl was going to get involved in *her* adventure. I scrambled onto the arm of the chair beside Wren. "There was magic in that song," I warned her. "Nothing bad, but it was meant to prod people and make them want to rescue the prince."

"I know," Wren said. "I could feel it. I knew those feelings were coming from outside me. But the prince—if he didn't run away, if he's a prisoner of goblins, or worse, *somebody* has to help him. She *is* right."

The man beside her shrugged, thinking Wren had been talking to him. "True enough," he said. "But we have to take the cows up to the high pastures, and there's cheese to be made. And before you know it, we'll have to start haying, and after the hay there's the grain harvest, and then the plums and apples, and the Royal Cheese Fair…they can't expect farmers to go off adventuring."

Wren wasn't even listening. She shoved back her chair and stood up.

"Excuse me," she said politely. "I'll be back in a moment."

She went out onto the veranda. I followed, and we both stood peering up and down the muddy lane.

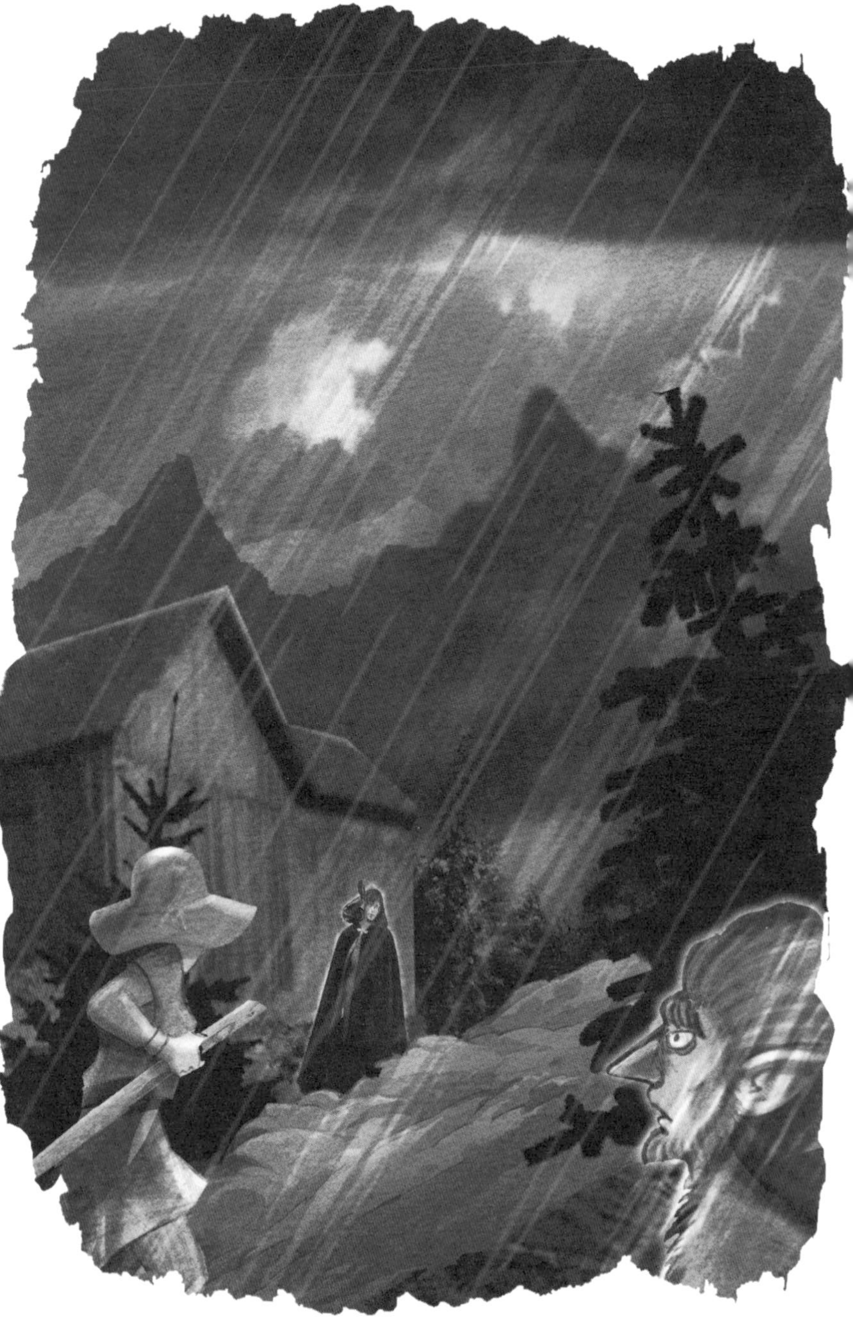

No Rookfeather. Not even any boot prints in the muck.

"She can't have gone far," Wren said. Without a thought for the rain, she ran, staggering a bit as the mud sucked at her feet. I ran after her, down the lane in the direction the minstrel would have to go if she was leaving the village.

"Did the minstrel go past here?" I stopped to ask Toby as we passed her again.

The dog opened one eye and yawned. "No. No minstrels."

"Wren!" I called, but she had stopped at the next barn. And there was Rookfeather, leaning against the wall as if she had been waiting for us. She wasn't nearly as wet as Wren and I were, I noticed as I trotted up to join them.

"Good afternoon," the minstrel said.

"How come *you're* not looking for the prince?" Wren demanded. "It's all very well saying the queen wanted you to find a hero, but why aren't you trying to rescue Liasis yourself?"

"Who says I'm not?" Rookfeather said. "I am. In my own way. At the moment, that involves finding a hero."

"Well," said Wren grimly. "I'm not much of a hero. But it doesn't seem like anyone else is going to do anything. And someone has to. I don't even know where to start. But I'll go."

"If someone did want to find Prince Liasis," the minstrel said, looking up at the thick gray clouds as though what she was saying wasn't really all that important, "the best place to start would be the track that runs north from King's Town into the wilderness and winds its way out of the mountains, down into the Wild Forest."

Most goblin clans live in the mountains, since they like tunnels and caves, but, in those days, a few lived right in the Forest itself.

"You mean we should follow the trail of that goblin band people were talking about," I said.

Wren looked at me and raised an eyebrow. I shrugged. "Rookfeather can see me," I explained, and I gave the minstrel a stern look. "Following those goblins is what the Twenty-Seven Royal Knights are supposed to have done, and no one's heard from them since."

"Ah," said Rookfeather, "but the kidnapper of the prince might have been expecting the Twenty-Seven Knights to follow the goblin trail, and he might have been prepared for them. A hero, on the other hand . . . it can be difficult to recognize a hero, sometimes. You should know that, Torrie."

Somehow, I wasn't surprised that she knew my name.

"Hm," Wren said. "Firstly, how do you know the prince was kidnapped, and didn't just run away to play the fiddle? Secondly, the trail of those goblins is a couple of weeks old by now, and it'll be older still by the time I get there, because it'll take me at least three days to get to King's Town from here, and that's if I take the straight road and don't stop to sell anything in the villages along the way. And thirdly, it sounds to me as though what you really want is someone to go ahead of you, in case whoever took the prince set some traps or is planing an ambush for anyone who comes to rescue him. Something must have happened to the knights, after all."

Rookfeather grinned, and again I caught that flash of sharp eyeteeth. "Liasis is not in the least musical. He did not run away to become any kind of musician. And following the trail of that goblin band *will* lead you to him. But why would you think I need anyone to spring traps for me, young Wren?"

For the first time since I had known her, Wren got angry.

"You can play games and sing sad songs," she said, "but isn't anybody thinking of the prince? Or his parents?"

"You're right," the minstrel said. "I'm sorry. I shouldn't make fun of you. No, I'm not expecting you to go ahead to run into all the traps for me. I don't believe there will be any left."

"You mean the Royal Knights will already have been caught by them all," I said.

"Perhaps," Rookfeather agreed, without looking the least guilty about it. "But if someone was expecting that the Twenty-Seven Knights would follow, and was prepared for that, let's just say he might be expecting a minstrel to follow, as well. But a pedlar? Not a pedlar. What do pedlars have to do with princes and goblins?"

"Nothing," said Wren.

"There you are, then," Rookfeather said.

I didn't think she had proved anything.

Wren, however, seemed to feel it was a good argument. She shrugged, as though she were agreeing to some little thing that didn't matter much. "All right, then. I'll see what I can do. Because it seems to me that everyone in this whole kingdom is just sitting around waiting for someone else to act. And Liasis might just as well be an orphan, like me, for all the help his family's being. Or their friends," she added pointedly.

It was the minstrel's turn to shrug.

"That remains to be seen," Rookfeather said. "But when you find the prince you'll need to…" She hesitated and put a hand to her head, the way you might if a sudden headache struck you, and then she took a deep breath and rubbed her eyes. For a moment, she looked ill, her face gray. "I'll say it another way," she muttered to herself. "I may tell you this much, I think." She hesitated again, and then went on slowly, picking her words with care. "You may not recognize the prince when you find him. But you may be his best hope to bring him back to himself. And when you do find him, this might be useful."

Out of her pocket she took a tightly folded scrap of red silk, and passed it to Wren. It looked like it could have been torn from her sleeve. Wren unfolded it.

"Careful!" said Rookfeather sharply, stretching out an arm to shield it from the wind.

Wren and I both peered at what was wrapped in the silk. A couple of scales, a bit of cobweb, and a single pale hair. The cobweb had an unpleasant, rotten sort of smell to it, and so did the scales. I wrinkled my nose. We both looked up, puzzled.

"Useful?"Wren asked. "How?"

"I'm sure you'll understand when you need to." Rookfeather offered Wren her hand to shake. "Good luck to you." She gave me her hand too, and then she hitched the strap of her harpsack higher on her shoulder and stepped out into the rain, making for the steep path that led down out of Hampstead's high valley, past the waterfalls and into the lower vales.

Wren folded the silk up tightly and put it in her innermost pocket. "That was really…strange," she said, as we trudged back towards the inn. She rested her hand on my shoulder, and a bit of her weight, too, because she had left her staff in the inn.

"I think," I grumbled, as the mud splashed up past my knees, "that Rookfeather's a sorcerer. They tend to get like that."

"Like what?" Wren asked.

"Full of their own importance. All cryptic and mysterious and letting on they know more than they're saying. Of course, often they do, and often they have a good reason for not telling people everything. But still...it's very annoying."

Wren looked back over her shoulder. "Torrie, she's gone!"

I looked, too. There was not a sign of Rookfeather anywhere, and unless she was running like a racehorse, she wouldn't have reached the path that led down by the waterfalls yet.

"Maybe she went into a barn," I said. But I didn't believe it. She probably *was* a sorcerer. And on top of that, she definitely was *not* entirely human.

"Well, sorcerer or not, I wish she'd explained a bit more. Why did she have to warn me I wouldn't recognize the prince? I've never met him before in my life. And what did she mean, bring him back to himself? Is she saying he's lost his memory? That'll make finding him even harder, when I don't even know what he looks like."

"Maybe that hair she gave you is his," I suggested.

Wren looked thoughtful. "Could you make some sort of prince-finding spell with it?"

"I wouldn't know how," I said, wondering if perhaps Wren could. "And what about that foul-smelling bit of cobweb, and the scales?"

"We'd better leave it all alone for now," Wren said. "Maybe it will make more sense later on."

I nodded. "I certainly hope so."

The rain began to pour down harder than ever.

"What have I done, Torrie?" Wren asked suddenly. "I know I

said I wanted to do something more than just wander around selling ribbons and buttons—but *this*!" She tried to laugh and didn't quite manage it. "Shouldn't heroes start off with something smaller? You know, rescuing kittens from trees?"

"Kittens, princes…" I waved my hand in the air.

"They're not the same," Wren said sternly, but her voice was a bit steadier. Of course she was nervous, more than a little daunted by what she had just agreed to do. Anyone but a fool or a madman would have been. However, that didn't mean she was going to give up, like the useless hero in the song Rookfeather had sung. Real heroes know being afraid sometimes is part of the job. "One step at a time, I suppose. I'll have to buy supplies for the wilderness."

"Cheese," I said. "Oatmeal. Butter, dried meat and fruit. It'll take us at least a few weeks to get out of the mountains, depending on which way the goblins went…" and Wren couldn't exactly trot along as fast as a band of goblins, "…and we don't know how far into the Wild Forest we'll have to go after that."

"Fish-hooks would come in handy…I need a new pair of socks…" Wren ticked items off on her fingers. "*Forth the dauntless hero rode…*" She quoted part of an old ballad. "Or walked, in my case. *Her trusty…quarterstaff…in hand.*"

"And a new pair of socks in her pocket," I sang, although, as various people have told me, I really shouldn't.

"I don't know the first thing about tracking goblins, Torrie."

"I do," I said. "But that's the easy part."

Chapter Four

In which Liasis begins his captivity

You're probably wondering what had been happening to Prince Liasis since he was dropped over the castle wall. Well, all the pleasant spring days were wasted on him. While Wren and Ash were wandering around the valleys of High Morroway, heading towards me, Hampstead-Above-The-Falls, and Rookfeather, Liasis was enduring a long, horrible journey in that sack.

He wasn't even sure how long it had been—days, then a week, but he might have missed a couple of days or counted them twice. It was hard to remember. He grew slow and sluggish without any food. They didn't even open the sack to give him a drink; they just dipped a corner of it in some water once in a while, and he swallowed what he could. Although at first he struggled to force the knot at the top of the sack open with his blunt nose, or to tear a hole in the tough cloth with his fangs, he had to give up as his body grew weaker. Still, whenever something pressed against the sack, he struck at it, hoping it was his captor's hand, and hoping he was poisonous. Probably he wasn't, because his aim improved as he grew more used to his new body, and once he had the satisfaction of hearing someone yelp as his fangs connected and he smelled blood. But it was only a yelp of pain and annoyance, not the panicked yelling of someone bitten by an adder.

Maybe goblins were immune to snake venom. The person he bit was probably a goblin. There were goblins all around, traveling with the man on the horse. He had to listen to their cackling laughter and their endless bickering, day after day. Snakes don't really have ears; they just feel vibrations through the ground, but of course, Liasis wasn't quite a proper snake. He could hear, though everything sounded strange and did seem to rumble around in his skull. From the goblins' talk, he learned that the man was named Abastor, and that he was a sorcerer.

Somehow, Liasis was not very surprised about that. What was surprising was that goblins would work for a human. They even called him "Lord Abastor," as though he was their ruler. But the prince could never forget that someone in the castle had thrown the bespelled net over him, transforming him and handing him over to the sorcerer. It was obviously not only goblins that Lord Abastor had working for him. Or was he working for someone in the castle?

It was all very worrying. But at least Liasis knew that the king would have sent the Twenty-Seven Royal Knights after him.

Before long, he would hear the sounds of battle, the whistle of arrows and the swish of swords, goblin squeals and Morrowaian war cries… He would be rescued. He had to believe that.

Liasis had faith in the knights, but the truth is that goblins can jog along at a good speed for ten or twelve hours without tiring, and the sorcerer's horse was only carrying him, not a lot of armor and supplies. The horses of the knights, on the other hand, were carrying people wearing coats of mail, as well as lots of weapons and supplies. Mail, which is made of thousands of iron rings linked together, isn't as heavy as the plate armor that humans made in later centuries, but it's still pretty heavy, as any knight or warhorse will tell you. Especially if you're climbing mountains in it. On top of that, it was easy to guess that Abastor and the goblins were traveling on narrow, dangerous, little-used tracks, where twenty-seven big warhorses would have to pick their footing very carefully. It was going to be difficult for anyone coming to the rescue to catch up, and Liasis began to realize this. Nevertheless, every now and then Abastor did send a goblin or two back as scouts, to look for the knights.

"And don't get lost like that idiot Treadle," he shouted at a scout, as the goblins made camp one morning (goblins travel at night and sleep during the day). "I told him to stay near the castle on that first night, to see if anyone followed right away, and he still hasn't caught up."

"Thimble," a goblin corrected him. "It was Thimble, my lord."

"Whatever," Abastor said.

"Maybe they caught him," another goblin suggested nervously.

"If he was stupid enough to get caught, he's no great loss," the sorcerer retorted. "Off you go, er, you, Fleabag."

"Fleabane," the goblin muttered, but only after the tread of Lord Abastor's heavy boots had moved away. "Betcha Thimble didn't get caught. He's so stupid, I betcha he never found Morroway Castle again at all."

"He probably went right by without seeing it. He's way down in Erythroth by now, wondering where the mountains have gone."

Liasis thought by then that it was about two weeks since he had been kidnapped, but he wasn't sure. The air had grown terribly cold, and he could hardly think, let alone move. When his mind seemed to be working at all, he decided that they must be crossing some very high pass, and that they were far from any part of the mountains that he knew. Even the daylight was cold, when the band stopped to sleep, and he wondered if he would start to hibernate, the way snakes did in winter, or just die if it got any colder.

But the air grew rapidly warmer over the next couple of night-time marches, and Liasis was sure the mountains were behind them. He began to hope that now, away from the steep and dangerous trails, the knights might catch up. But Lord Abastor must have thought of that, too. While the goblins slept away the daylight hours, the sorcerer paced about, rustling in leaves or crunching on dead twigs. He muttered spells, and occasionally seemed, from the whittling and chopping sounds and the scent of sappy wood, to be carving things on trees. Sometimes he laughed and seemed very pleased with himself.

But one day, more than a week after they had left the mountains, something changed. The air smelled and tasted of mud and water, lots of water. Insects whined and hummed in the air; redwings sang. The horse's hooves splashed and squelched, while the goblins laughed and yipped and pattered through shallow water.

Then it suddenly grew very dark, and the sounds echoed, as though they were inside a building.

And finally, finally, the mouth of the sack was untied.

Liasis couldn't blink; he had no eyelids. He stared, blinded for a moment by what seemed like the glare of a furnace, but then he realized it was only a torch. His eyes simply were not used to light unfiltered by the sack. His tongue flickered, and he tasted the air: damp stone, a sweating human who smelled like a sweating horse, dirty, reeking goblin, and, distantly, fresh air. Quick as thought, Liasis swarmed up the side of the sack and launched himself out. He landed with a thump and began slithering for his life. Unfortunately, he was weak and slow from so long without food or exercise.

"Stop him, you fools!" Abastor shouted, and a goblin slammed at the prince with a club. The blow missed, which was just as well, or this story would have ended right then.

"Don't hurt him!" And then Abastor roared, "*Karchichek!*" A shower of red and white sparks flared along the ceiling and floated gently to the floor like burning snowflakes. In that brighter light, Liasis could see that he wasn't in a natural cave, but in a large, pillared hall carved out of solid rock. He could also see a forest of gray goblin feet, all knobbly joints, with dirty toenails like dog's claws.

"Hah!" squealed a goblin, and she seized Liasis and swung him dangling into the air. "Got him, sir!" She was all grins and bobbing, anxious-to-please bows as she offered the squirming prince to the sorcerer. "What'll I do with him? Can we eat him?"

"What did I just say, Bobbin?"

"Not to hurt him, sir. But if we kill him quick, he won't be hurt. And then we can eat him."

"No one is to eat him. Did you all hear that?"

There was a chorus of goblin muttering: "Yes, sir." "Yes, Lord Abastor."

"If anyone eats him, I'll feed that goblin his or her own ears for dessert."

The goblins giggled and hissed. That was the sort of thing they found amusing.

"Bobbin, since you caught him, I'll put you in charge. You're now Chief Snake Guard."

The skinny little goblin sniffed, as if she didn't think much of her new title. Liasis twisted around and sank his fangs into Bobbin's hand. She screeched, but she didn't let go.

"Oooh, lookit the Chief Snake Guard!"

"The Snake Guard needs someone to guard her from the snake!"

"He's biting me, he's biting me, sir! Can't I bite him back, just a little?"

"No. Take him and throw him into the Pit. He won't be able to get out of there. And give him something to eat."

"Don't know what princes eat, sir," the goblin complained.

"Never ate a prince, neither."

"Princes eat lark's eggs and roast swan," said another goblin wisely.

"An' marzipan an' whipped cream an' candied violets."

"And…"

"Where am I supposed to get that sort of thing?" wailed Bobbin. Liasis would have laughed, if she hadn't been so nearly choking him.

"Idiots!" said the sorcerer. "He's a snake. A garter snake.

He eats slugs and worms, and frogs if he's lucky. Go on, Thimble—Spool—whatever your name is. Take him to the Pit before he gets away again. And I'm holding you responsible if anything bad happens to him."

"Why, my lord?" Bobbin whined, sucking the blood off her hand. "Why does it matter if something bad happens to the stupid prince?"

"Because I gave my word he wouldn't be harmed," Abastor said pompously. "And, unlike you, I have a sense of honor, and I keep my word."

"Oooh, the high and mighty goblin lord has honor," muttered Bobbin, as she slouched off down a narrow tunnel, clutching Liasis the way he'd seen toddlers clutching some battered toy. "Huh. Us goblins wouldn't know anything about that, not at all."

"You're not very respectful of your lord," Liasis said. His snake's voice was soft and breathy, and he didn't really expect the goblin to answer, but he thought it was worth a try. Goblins were a type of Old Thing, he knew, and in all the tales he'd heard, Old Things could understand animals.

"Abastor's not my lord," the goblin said sullenly, not seeming at all surprised at being spoken to. "He just came along last fall and told us he was. And when Snip and Snag—our chiefs—told him he wasn't, he turned 'em into swallows. Swallows! All black and shiny and fast in the sky. And they flew away south, and we haven't seen 'em since."

"That's too bad," Liasis said sympathetically.

"Yeah. I mean, we're goblins. He says he's going to give us

a whole kingdom to plunder and loot in the end, but what's the point of that? I mean, if it's just ours, where's the fun? No sneaking, no stealing, no being cunning and sly."

"I see what you mean," Liasis said. The goblin's grip was relaxing as she brooded on her wrongs, and he thought he might be able to slip free, if he just wiggled…

"None of that!" Bobbin pinched his tail. "I don't want to end up any flittery, twittery birdbrain!"

"But you don't want to spend the rest of your life some enchanter's servant, either, do you?"

"No way! Goblins should be ruled by goblins. And His Lordship Abastor sent poor Thimble off scouting just after we left your castle, and everybody knows he's got no sense of direction at all. And when he never came back, the Great Goblin Lord said one more or less didn't make any difference. He wouldn't let me go look for him."

"So why not get back at him by letting me go?"

"You getting away doesn't get rid of Abastor. You get away and I'll be eatin' my own ears and then flying south, a deaf bird." She looked thoughtful. "Do birds have ears?"

"There wouldn't be any point to all their singing if they didn't."

All the time he talked to Bobbin, Liasis was trying to memorize the twists and turns of their route. The goblin den looked like it had probably begun as a series of natural caves, eroded by water and ice, which someone had started to carve into a palace. Pillars and arches had been sculpted into the walls and ceiling, doorways made square, and flights of stairs carved to connect the many small rooms. There were even a few deep, arched windows, although many of them were covered up with ragged mats woven from reeds. In some places, rainwater dripping through cracks had begun to cover the carving with crusts and icicles of new stone, so whoever had tried to turn the cave into a palace had obviously done so long ago. And they probably hadn't been goblins, who don't understand beauty.

"Here's the Pit," said Bobbin, after pattering down a last narrow flight of stairs. "You behave yourself, Prince Snaky, and I'll get you some nice worms."

Liasis couldn't see any pit from where he was, just a rock wall made shiny from seeping water, and a thin shaft of light striking down from a hole in the ceiling.

"How about some bread and cheese?" Liasis asked desperately. "Since we're friends and all. We are friends, aren't we, Bobbin?"

"Don't know why we should be," the goblin said. "And you might as well ask for violet's eggs and candied swans as bread and cheese, around here. All the good loot we took from High Morroway will go to His Lordship Abastor, and he'll dole it out when he says we deserve it, which won't be very often. Bread and cheese and corned beef and beer—it isn't the ones that do the raiding and take the risks that eat the feasts any more. Worms is what he said, and worms is what you'll get. But I'll make sure they're nice fresh ones," she added.

And Liasis made himself say, "Thanks. If there's ever anything I can do for you…"

"If I ever need a midnight snake, y' mean?" Bobbin said, with a hideous grin. "Midnight snake, midnight snack!" Her curving yellow fangs leaned every which way, like a jumbled, broken-down fence. Liasis forced out a raspy, snaky chuckle.

"Here we are, cosy Pit. Don't get lost." Bobbin snickered again, and dropped him onto a pile of crackling brown leaves. As soon as had his breath back, he looked around.

It was a pit. The Pit. It had been cut down into the stone floor of the cave, and was about the size and shape of a barrel. Probably it had been made for storage, or even as a very small cistern to hold water. The sides were smooth gray stone that he couldn't get a grip on with his rough belly scales, no matter how quickly he rushed at the walls. The floor, where it wasn't covered with drifted leaves, was a bit uneven, and in the lower side there was a puddle of water about an inch deep.

Liasis gave up trying to scale the walls of the Pit and slithered into the puddle instead, letting the cool water soothe his bruises. He opened his mouth and drank, feeling as though the water was soaking into his dried-out body as he gulped it down. It tasted a bit like mud, but it washed the foul tang of Bobbin-blood out of his mouth.

THE LIGHT FROM THE SMALL SHAFT in the ceiling was growing dimmer with evening when there was a pattering of bare goblin feet and Bobbin came back, to stand over the edge of the Pit, peering down at him. It was the first time he'd had a good look at her. She was a smallish goblin, gray-skinned, with thin gray hair all over. It grew quite thickly on her head and shoulders, like a lion's mane. She wore a kilt of rat-skins around her waist, their tails making a fringe at her knee. A long, stone-bladed knife was stuck into her rope belt like a sword. A leather purse with a draw-string at the top dangled from the belt. Liasis wondered what a goblin would want to keep in a purse, and then decided he really didn't want to know. Eye of newt and toe of frog, probably. Just in case she got hungry and needed a snack.

"Here you go, Snaky-Prince," she said cheerfully. "Suppertime."

She opened her cupped hands, which were black with mud, and a dozen wriggling pink earthworms showered over Liasis.

His first reaction was to roar in disgust and cover his head with his hands, but he couldn't do either, so he just slithered back to the pile of dry leaves and flicked his tongue.

"Typical human. I do all that digging and he can't even say thanks," Bobbin muttered. "Huh. Not much to choose from between you and Abastor, is there?"

"Ah…sorry," said Liasis. "You just took me by surprise. I mean, there's so many of them."

"Well, maybe if you eat a lot you'll grow big and strong. You can grow up into a big python or something, and swallow Abastor."

"I don't think it works that way."

"You can at least try!" said the goblin angrily. And she stomped away, leaving Liasis glumly thinking that…he was very, very…hungry.

Liasis watched the worms wriggling around on the stone floor of the Pit for a while. There wasn't really anywhere for them to go, not a crack or a cranny they could squeeze into. Most of them were disappearing under his bed of leaves.

Finally, wishing he could shut his eyes and not see what he was doing, he thrust his head under the leaves. Trying not to taste it, he picked up a worm in his mouth.

The worm wriggled frantically. It tasted of mud, and felt tough and slimy, like gristle in beef.

He swallowed it anyway.

WORMS ARE HEALTHY, Liasis told himself. Robins eat worms, and look how plump and cheerful they are. Worms are good for me.

He couldn't make himself believe it, and yet he kept eating them, day after day after day. It was important to keep his strength up. The Twenty-Seven Royal Knights of Morroway might be slowed down by Abastor's spells, but they wouldn't be stopped. Pretty soon they'd be charging into this cave with their helmets gleaming and their blades hungry for goblin blood. He'd have to make sure they didn't hurt Bobbin, because, in her own peculiar way, she was trying to be nice....

There was one flaw in all his hopes. Liasis tried to avoid thinking about it, but as he lay there digesting his horrible, slimy, slithering meals of earthworms, the thought kept creeping back. If Lord Abastor could turn him into a snake, what else could he do?

Two flaws. How on earth was he going to let the knights know who he was?

Day after day after day, and no rescue came. Bobbin began to seem like good company. On the very first day, Liasis had scratched a tiny mark on the stone floor of his prison with his fang, and since then he had made a new mark every morning. One week. Two. Lord Abastor took no interest in him. In all the stories Liasis had ever read about captive princes, their captors spent a lot of time gloating over them as they languished in chains in damp and lightless cells. Lord Abastor couldn't seem to be bothered. Only once did he come to check on the prince in the Pit.

The goblins' lord was a tall man, with curly black hair tied back from his face, a tidy, gray-streaked black beard, brown skin, and bright green eyes. His face was narrow, and his nose long and thin with a bit of a hump to it, the sort of nose humans call aquiline, which means "eagle-like." He dressed in leather trousers and a leather jerkin, like a huntsman. He also wore a black cloak lined with purple velvet, which looked very dramatic, but not so practical for living in damp caves.

"Nobody's eaten you yet, I see," the sorcerer said. "Heh heh." It wasn't much of a villainous laugh. Any actor in the poorest wandering theater troupe could have done better.

"Go soak your head," Liasis hissed.

"Not exactly good manners for a prince, but I suppose that's to be expected from a backwater like High Morroway."

Liasis reared his head up. "You can hear me! I thought that humans wouldn't be able to understand me!" That meant if he could get away from this place and find the knights…

Lord Abastor gave him a narrowed-eyed look. "They can't."

"But you can." Liasis slumped down on the leaves again. "Because you're a sorcerer?"

"No." The sorcerer looked down his nose.

"Because it was you who cast the spell?" He needed to know. He needed to know who he would have to find, to be able to explain that he wasn't really a snake and needed help.

"No. And I didn't come here to play 'Yes or No, Black or White'."

"Gloating isn't very honorable, *Lord* Abastor."

"I *came*," the sorcerer said, "to see how you were doing," He hesitated. "You're being looked after well?" As though Abastor were the host and Liasis his guest.

"Bobbin makes sure I have lots of worms, yes," said Liasis sarcastically.

"Good, good. They seem to be agreeing with you. Your scales are nice and glossy, and I think you've grown an inch or so."

"Perhaps you should try them."

Abastor snorted and turned on his heel.

"Hey, wait!" Liasis couldn't shout, but the hissing, breathy words were as forceful as he could make them. "You promised I wouldn't be harmed. I heard you. Who threw that snake-charm over me? Who made you promise?"

"A gentleman never tells on a lady," the sorcerer called back as he left.

"What lady?" Liasis demanded, but there was no answer.

Not his stepmother. It couldn't have been Demansia, so gentle and kind. Or was Abastor lying about the person being a woman? Even if he was, that didn't help. Liasis couldn't think of anyone, female or male, in the whole castle who hated him enough to help turn him into a snake and kidnap him.

Lord Abastor never came to see him again. Two weeks since he was put into the Pit. Three. Almost a month.

A month of eating worms.

"Hey, Snaky-Prince!"

Liasis looked up to see Bobbin squatting on the lip of the Pit, her long-clawed toes curled around the edge.

"What?" he asked, sounding as cheerful and interested as he could.

"I got a surprise for you. The thing is—you're a snake. You eat worms and frogs and stuff. Right?"

"Not if I can help it," said Liasis.

"Yeah, but maybe you can't help it. What I want to know is, do you eat toads?"

"Do I have to?" Liasis asked, feeling a knot in his stomach. Toads had eyes. They would look at him. True, he ate beef and mutton, but they had always been killed quickly, and they were cooked. To slowly swallow something that was still alive and was looking at him...again, he almost found out whether or not snakes could throw up. "I don't think I can eat a toad," he said. "I'm sorry, Bobbin. I know you mean well. But...could I have earthworms, please? Or even slugs?"

"Hah, no, lucky for you, these toads aren't for eating. I jus' wanted to make sure you weren't going to come over all hungry and gobble them up. Lord Abastor's magic showed him some friends of yours was coming. He didn't expect that— thought he'd got 'em trapped where they couldn't bother him. Someone messed up his spells, I guess. Anyhow, he jus' got back from meeting them. He really wasn't in a good mood. He's been at his old tricks again."

And Bobbin pulled out a basket from behind her back.

"Look out!" she shrieked, jumping to her feet. "It's raining toads!" And while she danced around the edge of the Pit, shaking down toads and giggling, Liasis darted for shelter underneath his pile of leaves.

Toads thumped and plopped around him.

Over two dozen of them.

Twenty-seven, to be exact.

CHAPTER FIVE

In which we find a trap

Wren wasn't a person to waste time once she had made up her mind. Three days later we reached King's Town and Morroway Castle. Near the castle I found the trail of the goblin band, even though it was over two weeks since they went by. Goblins can't resist smashing and breaking as they go. The trail of trampled crops and wounded trees was easy to follow.

In only a few more days we had left High Morroway behind and were into the wilderness. North of High Morroway, the mountain range is wide. Its peaks rise sharp-edged, crowned with white snows that never melt, even in the hottest summers, hiding countless valleys and ravines. You can climb and scramble among the rocks all day, up and down, following paths as crooked as a child's scribbles, and travel only the distance a crow might fly while you drank a cup of tea.

For several weeks we traveled without seeing a single human, or any goblins either. We hiked through high valleys under pine trees, or crawled along steep slopes where loose rock slid away beneath our feet, rattling and clattering for what seemed like hours as it fell, before landing in some churning river far below. Sometimes we had to cross those rivers, but luckily the goblins seemed to know where they were going, and their trail always led to a safe ford, where we could cross without being swept away.

In the lower valleys, summer was no doubt beginning, with roses sweet in the hedgerows, but it was cold up where we were. The worst part was when we went over a high, knife-sharp ridge where the air was thin and made Ash and Wren pant and gasp; the climb was so steep that Wren's twisted foot was rubbed raw. That night we could see our breath, as though it were winter, and the stars burned far more brightly than they seem to lower down. I bandaged Wren's bloody foot with a poultice of alder bark and wintergreen from the supplies she carried.

The next morning we started at dawn, mostly because we were so cold we hadn't slept much anyway.

"Ad-v-ventures-s," Wren said, wrapped in a blanket with her teeth chattering, "are v-vastly over-r-rated-d."

"W-we h-haven't-t h-had any y-y-yet," I answered.

That was soon to change.

It didn't take us long to both warm up and cheer up. The sun climbed over the peaks and the chill morning mists burned off into a golden day. The path ahead looked like a dead end, though. The narrow ravine we were following got narrower and narrower, until it ended against a steep slope of tumbled rock.

"There's been a landslide,"Wren said, looking up at the cliffs.

"And fairly recently, too." She pointed to where a clump of spiky grass lay flattened, sticking out from under a slab of stone. "I don't like it," I said, looking at the cliffs as well. "Something doesn't feel right."

"Landslides happen a lot in the mountains," said Wren.

"Especially after rain."

"Those cliffs look pretty solid to me, and anyway, it hasn't rained recently." I listened, with my head tipped a little to one side. There was almost...no, maybe I was imagining it.

"You don't think this is one of those traps Rookfeather said we wouldn't run into?" Wren's mouth was set in a grim line.

"It...it doesn't look like anyone was caught under it. Does it?"

We both gave it a long, worried look. There were lots of odd, dusty lumps and edges, but they all seemed to be stones, not legs or helmets or horses' feet.

Ash snorted. "If there were bodies, you'd smell them."

Animals are very down to earth about such things.

"True," I agreed, but I didn't tell Wren what the pony had said. "Can we climb over it, Wren?" What I meant, of course, was could she climb over? Her bad foot was really hurting her that day, I could tell.

"We're going to have to," Wren said.

Ash's ears went flat to his head. "I'm not scrambling up that," he said. "I'm not a goat."

"It'll be all right," I told him. "We'll lead you. Just watch where you put your hooves."

We picked a way over the treacherous loose rock. Some of it was fine gravel, but quite a lot of it was slabs of stone, which tilted and rocked or even slid beneath us. I went first, testing the footing, and Wren followed, leading the pony. Pebbles rattled and pattered away below us.

That noise I had decided was just my imagination wasn't. All of a sudden I could hear, faintly, as though it was coming from under the rocks, a deep, deep humming, wandering from note to note like a tone-deaf giant trying to remember a lullaby. I could feel it, too, in the soles of my feet and inside my chest. It was not a comfortable feeling.

"Is the ground shaking?" Wren asked, and that was when half the mountain fell down around us. At least it seemed like half at the time.

Ash whinnied and whirled about, leaping like a goat as the slope of loose stone and scree swept around him. The rock beneath my feet shrugged and heaved. Wren grabbed me, trying to keep her balance and I grabbed her, trying to keep mine. The ground shook. The air shook. It was like being inside a peal of thunder. We were deaf from the roar of it, blind from the dust, but I could feel that we were falling, then sliding, being pushed along as if by a river.

Clutching one another, we crouched, trying to keep from falling down flat. We both felt just as if we *were* being swept away by water and that if our heads went under, it was all over. But that didn't work. Our feet went out from under us and we slid and banged and tumbled and somehow never quite ended up buried and crushed beneath the weight of the cliff.

Then the thunder faded. Stinging shards of gravel pelted us, but the ground wasn't moving any more. I raised my head, blinking grit out of my tearing eyes, and saw a chunk of stone bigger than me go bouncing over us. Wren pushed my head back down again, trying to protect me.

"It's all right," I said, sitting up. "I think it's over."

"Is it?"Wren asked. "My ears are still ringing."

"So are mine. But nothing seems to be moving. That's probably a good sign."

"And we're not under a ton of rock. That's a better one."

Actually, we were back on the trail at the bottom of the ravine. There was an occasional clatter from behind, but that was all. Wren started coughing. I pounded her on the back, which didn't help much, although it raised a large cloud of dust from her cloak. Somehow she had kept a grip on her staff. We both struggled to our feet, bruised and battered, and looked around.

After a moment, Wren said, "I think we're going to have to find another way over."

The second rockslide had completely blocked the ravine. There were huge blocks balanced atop jagged corners, round boulders kept from tumbling only by a pebble beneath their edge. Neither Wren nor Ash was going to be able to climb over that.

Ash! I looked around wildly. Was he—no, there he was, looking a bit frantic and white around the eyes, his coat all floury with dust, but otherwise unharmed. He snorted and trotted over to nose at Wren for comfort.

"Are you all right?" I asked, seeing that her hands were bleeding. So were mine, actually.

"I still have four legs," Ash answered me. "I don't know how."

"I'm fine," said Wren. "Although I think I've torn the seat of my trousers. How about you?"

"I'm not wearing any trousers," I pointed out. "Ouch." Wren grinned. "Well, I can darn my trousers tonight, but I think you'll have to deal with your own problems."

I checked. At least my behind was still decently covered with fur. It would have been very embarrassing to end up with bald patches. I would have had to borrow Wren's spare trousers, and they wouldn't have fit me at all.

"That," I said, "was a trap. Definitely."

"But we got out of it," Wren said, being serious again. "Somehow." She wiped dust off her face. "I didn't think people could just swim down rockslides like that."

"They can't," I said. "Not usually. We were meant to survive."

"Ah," said Wren. "How thoughtful. I suppose that means the knights survived too, and found a way around."

"It was probably meant to slow them down," I suggested, wondering if that could be right. It seemed too easy.

"It obviously didn't make them give up,"Wren agreed. "We haven't met them going back to King's Town. We just need to find how they went around."

I would have liked to find a way to end the spell that caused the landslide. There must have been some magical symbols carved somewhere, to anchor the spell, but I couldn't see any. Probably, I thought gloomily, they were buried under the rocks, where it would take wind and weather a good long time to wear them away, and where we couldn't get at them, either. If this was the Wild Forest, I found myself thinking…but it wasn't. A strong Old Thing of the mountains might have been able to wish the cliffs solid again and the heap of rocks stable, but there wasn't much I could do to stop the sorcerer's spell from making the cliffs crumble and the stones leap and dance under the next unlucky travelers to come by. All I could do was ask the next wild creature we saw to find an Old Thing, one of the powerful mountain spirits. Of course, when you're traveling with a human, the wild creatures tend to stay away from you, and so do most OldThings. I'd go look for someone who could help when we made camp, I decided. Right now, we needed to find a way out of the ravine.

We headed back the way we had come, feeling a bit stiff and hoping we wouldn't have to go all the way back to the high pass where we'd spent the night. After only a few hundred yards we found what we were looking for, something that was almost a path up the side of the ravine.

Notice I said *almost*.

"Did the knights really go this way?" Wren asked doubtfully.

I nodded and pointed where the uneven layers of rock in the cliff face made a sort of zigzag path. The few small, woolly plants were trampled and crushed, and, when we looked more

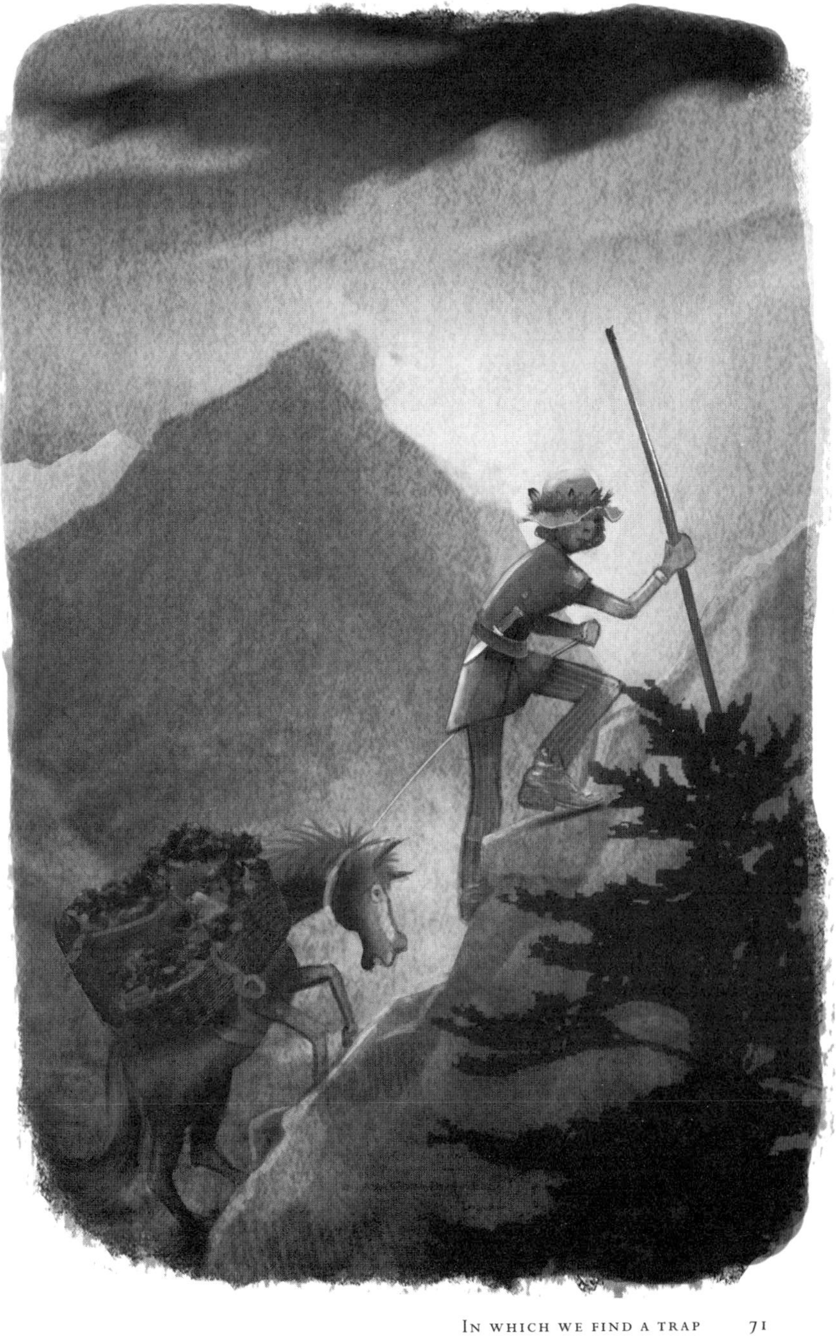

closely, we could see the scuffing of iron horseshoes on rock.

"Well, if twenty-seven warhorses climbed that, so can one pony." Wren tugged on Ash's rope. "Come on, boy."

I was still staring up the cliff. There were several dark cracks that looked like they could be caves, which is always a bit worrying in the mountains. You never know what might be living in them. If I was on my own it wouldn't matter, but the sorts of things that live in caves like that tend to look on humans as just another big, tasty animal. And now it seemed to me as if that landslide might have been *meant* to make us climb this cliff.

Ash didn't like it either. The pony balked. He planted his feet, braced himself against the rope, and laid back his ears.

"I'm not going up there," he said. "I can't. I won't."

"There's no other way out," I told him.

"I don't care. I'm not climbing up there. It's worse than the landslide."

"You don't have a choice."

"C'mon, Ash. Look." Wren rummaged around in one of his baskets and took out the dried-up heel of the last loaf of King's Town bread. "Tasty."

Ash stretched his neck out to sniff. "She's going to let me have bread? Real bread?"

"She wouldn't tease you," I said. "Go on."

Ash took a cautious step, and then another. I scrambled around Wren. I wanted to go first, to make sure the narrow ledges hadn't broken under a heavy horse's hooves.

Halfway up, Ash was dark with sweat and trembling with fear.

I was almost afraid to look up, to see how far we still had to climb, but I did. We were below one of those black cracks in the rock I had noticed earlier. A few yards further on I found myself climbing carefully over a litter of clean white bones, and the skulls and horns of sheep and chamois. There was only one predator in the mountains that made piles of bones like this beneath its lairs.

"Wren," I called back. "I think there's a—"

And that was when the griffin swooped down on us from the top of the cliff.

Have you ever seen one? Griffins aren't exactly Old Things, but they aren't ordinary animals either. They're the size of lions, and their bodies and back legs belong to a lion, but their head and front legs are those of a giant eagle. They have wings, too, and ears like a lynx, and they speak in human voices—which doesn't stop them eating humans once in a while, although griffins don't hunt them like dragons do.

I heard the rush of air, the swoosh of its wings, and smelled the heavy, cat-like smell of it. All I saw was a tawny blur as it dropped towards Wren.

She shouted, raising her staff. Ash reared, flailing with his front hooves. The stone beneath a rear hoof crumbled, and then, with a horrid, frantic scrabbling and a squeal, he was gone, his rope ripping free of Wren's hand. But if it hadn't, she'd have gone over too. There was a dreadful, solid *thump*, and a brief clatter of stones.

"*Ash!*" Wren screamed and flung herself down full length on the ledge, reaching after him.

I grabbed her, before she went over too, and for a moment we both lay there.

The griffin, a big female, circled the ravine and came back, wings beating heavily as she tried to hover, looking us over.

"Get away," I snarled at the beast. Wren hurled her staff like a spear. It struck the griffin on her feathery chest, but it was the head of the staff, not the spiky end. She coughed and dropped away out of sight below our ledge.

There was another nasty thump, and a squawk, and a very self-satisfied horsy snort.

Wren gasped and hurled herself forward again to peer over the edge. I quickly sat on her legs.

"Ash!" she cried, and started shaking. It was a moment before I realized it was with laughter. "Get back from the edge," I said sternly, and I tugged on her cloak until she sat up against the cliff. Then I crawled forward myself and peered down.

Ash hadn't plunged to his death after all. He'd slid down onto the ledge we had already climbed. He still ought to have broken a leg or two, which would have been the same thing. But he hadn't. He was fine.

And there was a faint, silvery noise humming in the air, like a distant bell. Even as I listened it died away. Sorcery, I thought. Some sorcery, protecting him...I stared at the fancy which hung on the breast-strap of his harness. A charm to keep him safe and well. It wouldn't have saved him if he'd fallen all the way down, but it had given him luck, kept him from breaking his legs in this short fall. There *was* real power in Wren's fancies.

The pony was swishing his tail and watching the griffin out of the corner of his eye. She was sitting bolt upright on the ledge a few yards away from him, a tawny yellow beast with dull-gold plumage, licking one hind foot like a cat and pretending to ignore him.

"Sneaking up on me," Ash said, when he saw me looking. "Nasty creature. I kicked her in the ribs. She'll think twice before she tries to catch a pony again."

"Good," I said weakly.

"Annoying animals," the griffin said, apparently speaking to her foot. "What makes them think one would want to eat a stringy old pony?"

"You dropped on us," I said accusingly. "What are we supposed to think?"

"Naturally one drops on them, to see what they're up to. Nasty creatures creeping up on one's eggs," the griffin said, now scratching behind her ear. "One should have eaten that wretched sorcerer, ruining a perfectly good path so that everyone and their furry servant tries to climb up this way."

"Servant?" I squawked, but Wren shushed me.

"The sorcerer with the goblins?" she asked. "Did the prince look all right?"

"One saw no princes."

"A boy, a prisoner!"

"One saw no young humans of any sort. One is not interested in young humans." The griffin sniffed and leapt into the air. She flapped over our heads, a bit stiffly, muttering, "Sorcerers and goblins and knights and OldThings. One did think this was a nice quiet place, but one is constantly disturbed and threatened. One's mate is still not able to hunt, after what those knights did to him. One might as well have chosen to nest on the highway."

She disappeared into the narrow mouth of the cave. Another griffin appeared, crouched on the ledge. He was smaller and brighter-colored, his fur coppery and his plumage gleaming like polished bronze, but one eye was swollen and crusted from a cut on the side of his head and he held a front leg curled up, its talons clenched. Of course he would have attacked the knights, defending his mate and their eggs when the warriors climbed up the cliff towards the lair, and of course the knights would have fought back. I sighed. There wasn't much I could do about it. At least the wounds didn't look infected and the griffin would still be able to fly, and even hunt again, though he was probably always going to limp. Like Wren.

Seeing the wounded griffin made me think. A landslide like the one in the ravine could have killed us. It should have killed us. But it hadn't, and it didn't seem like the knights had been badly harmed, either. And the griffins weren't really much of a threat to trained warriors. I wondered…were the unlucky griffins only supposed to make the knights *think* that was the sort of ambush they could expect? So the knights would underestimate the sorcerer and be completely taken by surprise when they rode into something worse?

I was going to have to keep a sharp lookout for trickier traps.

Wren was still staring up at the griffin's aerie. She only looked around when I climbed down to get her staff.

"So beautiful," she said. "Those huge wings…I wish I could fly."

"One wouldn't like it if you flew off and left one alone here halfway up a cliff," I said.

Wren laughed, but then looked thoughtful. "No boy with the sorcerer," she said. "I don't like the sound of that. You don't think they really did eat him?"

"No," I said firmly. "Probably the griffin didn't notice him."

The look Wren gave me said she didn't think that was very likely, but I thought the griffin was telling the truth.

"Maybe he really was hidden in a sack," I suggested.

"Disguised as potatoes. I hope that's it." Wren suddenly sat and slid down the cliff face to the lower ledge, terrifying me and making Ash throw up his head in alarm.

"Look at that!" She plucked something from the ground, dull gold in color, with a metallic sheen, and as long as her forearm. "A griffin feather." She couldn't have said "A diamond" with any more awe.

I handed her another and watched the way her face went remote and thoughtful and wondering as she stroked the two long feathers.

"You could make an interesting fancy with those," I suggested.

"Or something...wings...but that would take sorcery." Wren stowed the two griffin feathers in a basket, handling them as carefully as if they were made of glass. Then we gave Ash his bread and started, one careful step at a time, up the zig-zagging ledges once again. The male griffin had disappeared inside again, but the female watched us from the cave, her glaring, golden eyes unblinking.

"If you don't want people climbing past your door," I called down, once we were up on the windswept barrens over the cliff, "find a mountain spirit to get rid of the sorcerer's landslide spell for you."

I heard a rustle of wings, as if the griffin had given herself an indignant shake. "One does not," she said clearly, "need advice from a human's furry little pet."

Wren chuckled. Ash snickered. I snorted and gave the pony's rope a tug. "Come on, Ash. We domestic animals aren't wanted here."

"I don't think I have to obey pets," Ash said. "Ask Wren if I do, Torrie." He curled his lip wickedly at me in a horse-chuckle.

"The Old Thing is wise," the male griffin's voice said. "One will seek out the spirit of the high pass as soon as may be. Thank you."

"Wise," I said. "That's better."

"I don't know," said Ash. "If any of us were wise, we'd have stayed in High Morroway, where there's oats and cheese and bran-mash."

CHAPTER SIX

In which we take a prisoner

We only had to travel a mile or so along the barren, broken clifftop before we found an easy path back down to the main trail, where we picked up the goblins' track again. Two nights after we met the griffins, we camped in one of the lower valleys. Another day would see us out of the mountains. We had fallen even farther behind the goblins, but Wren never gave up hope that we would find the prince. I didn't either, but I did wonder what could have happened to the Twenty-Seven Knights. If we had to rescue them too… I fell asleep worrying, and woke up suddenly later that night. Wren had hold of me by my toe.

"Torrie!" she whispered, tweaking it yet again. "Wake up!"

"I'm awake, I'm awake!" I hissed. "What is it?"

"There's something sneaking around the camp. I heard it rustling in the heather on the slope up above us. I'm going to creep up and get behind it. You stay here in case I startle it down into the camp."

"Be careful," I said, getting up and crouching by the fire, which Wren had covered with pieces of turf to keep its embers going until the morning. Judging by the stars, dawn was an hour or so away. I yawned, and, in case I had to thump anything, I picked up a dead branch from the pile of firewood we'd collected for cooking our breakfast.

"Ash," I whispered, as Wren faded away into the night. "Wake up!"

The pony was asleep standing up, with his weight slouched on one hip. He snorted and looked around wildly.

"Wake up, quietly!" I whispered.

Ash flung his head up, nostrils flaring. "Goblin!" he said.

I sniffed, and caught a faint whiff. At least it smelled like only one.

A shriek tore the darkness. Something came stumbling and wailing down the heathery hillside above us. I yelled, kicking the sods off the fire. The glowing coals flared into new life as the air struck them. The goblin screeched and tried to change direction, but he fell flat on his rump. Wren leapt down behind him, brandishing her staff in one hand. With the other she grabbed him by the scruff of his neck and pulled him to his feet.

"I didn't do it!" he cried. "Wasn't me!"

"Wasn't you when?" I asked, and "What didn't you do?" demanded Wren.

The goblin shivered, wrapping his scrawny arms close about his body. "Didn't do it, whatever it was. Wasn't me." His eyes strayed to the fire, and he licked his lips, showing all his crooked, pointed fangs. Then he peered piteously up at Wren. "Hungry," he said hopefully. "Tasty bannock?"

"Have you been following us?" I demanded.

The goblin looked both panicked and sly, which is very difficult to do. "Maybe?" he said.

"You were following us!" Wren cried.

"No, no, not really. I was just—you were in front of me. Not my fault if stupid humans get in the way."

"Who are you calling stupid?" Wren asked. "If you're going to beg for food, you should at least flatter people."

"Who are you calling human?" I asked. "Look out!"

As the goblin whipped around and snapped at Wren I thumped him with my piece of firewood. He squeaked and crumpled up on the ground, unmoving.

Wren poked him carefully with the toe of her boot. "I think you knocked him out, Torrie."

"Talk about biting the hand that feeds you," I said.

"Well, I haven't fed him yet, unless you're counting the bannock he stole weeks ago in High Morroway. He is the same one, isn't he?"

"He's wearing skunk skins, at least."

"What should we do with him, Torrie? Do you think he's spying on us for whoever kidnapped the prince?"

"He might be," I said doubtfully. "Though he doesn't seem bright enough. Better tie him up before he wakes."

Wren had all sorts of useful odds and ends among her gear, and rope, of course, is one of those things that is always useful to take traveling in the mountains. I propped the goblin up against the trunk of a tree and tied him there while Wren fed the fire so that she had a bit of light to see by. In a moment or two the goblin groaned and opened his eyes.

"It wasn't me!" he said.

I started to say something, but Wren shook her head at me.

"We know," she said sympathetically. "What's your name?"

The goblin looked a bit surprised. "Thimble," he said suspiciously.

"We know you didn't do anything, Thimble," she said. "We only want to ask you a few questions."

"'Bout what?"

"About why you're following us," she said.

"And if you know anything about Prince Liasis," I added.

"Food first," said the goblin slyly. "Can't answer questions when I'm faint with hunger."

Wren unwrapped a cheese and sliced off a narrow sliver. Thimble watched the way a dog will watch someone holding a sausage, all his attention fixed on the hand holding the food.

"Answers first," Wren said sweetly, waving the paring of cheese.

Thimble smacked his lips a couple of times. He really did look very scrawny, even for a goblin.

"Lost," he muttered.

"What?" I asked.

"I got lost," he snarled. "Got sent off scouting to find out if the knights were after us, didn't I, and I got lost. 's not my fault. He should have known. I always get lost."

"So why were you following us?" Wren asked.

"You know where you're going, don' cha? I'm following you to get home. I'm not stupid."

Thimble suddenly let out a wail. Ash had been sneaking up behind Wren, and just then he stretched out his neck and curled his lips back, nipping the cheese out of her hand with his square yellow teeth.

"Ash!" Wren scolded, and the pony flicked his tail, looking innocent.

"Waste of good food, letting a goblin have it," he said with a snort.

"Hungry!" cried Thimble.

"Behave yourself," I told the pony. "We're trying to get him to cooperate."

"You can't trust a goblin," Ash said.

"We can't trust you either, obviously."

"I like cheese. Wren never gives me any."

"That's probably because horses aren't supposed to eat cheese. Look, go stand over on the other side and keep watch, why don't you?"

Ash sighed, blowing my fur every which way, and plodded off, standing rather too close on the other side of Thimble, with his ears folded threateningly back and his head lowered so his breath huffed on the goblin.

Wren cut another slice of cheese and waggled it enticingly. "The knights?" she prompted.

"The Royal Knights," Thimble said, pouting. "The ones looking for the prince."

"Ah," said Wren happily. "Now that's what we want to hear about." She poked a bit of cheese into Thimble's open mouth and patted him on the head, wiping her hand on the skirt of her tunic afterwards. "Now, who took the prince?"

Even with the cheese as a bribe, it took us a long time to find out what we wanted to know from Thimble. He really wasn't very bright, even for a goblin. Although he told us that the chief of his goblin band was a sorcerer named Lord Abastor, he couldn't tell us why Lord Abastor wanted the prince. But at least now we knew that the griffin *was* wrong and the prince *was* with the goblins we were following. And he didn't know where his band's home actually was, except that it wasn't in the mountains, and it was "kind of swampy."

"That's a big help," said Wren.

"Really?" Thimble grinned happily, a horrible sight. "Can I have lots of cheese, then?"

"You've had enough cheese," Wren said. "No more food till breakfast."

"Sun's coming up," said Thimble, sulking again. "It's breakfast time."

You'll have noticed one important fact about the prince that Thimble forgot to mention to us.

WREN MADE BANNOCK INSTEAD of porridge for breakfast, because she only had two wooden spoons and neither of us wanted to share our spoon with the goblin. We fed him and took our own breakfast up the hillside, so we could talk in private. Ash grazed closer and closer to the goblin, tearing at the grass right beside his toes, flicking his tail wickedly. Thimble curled himself up as small as he could get and sat with his eyes closed, as if not seeing the pony could somehow make him disappear.

"Oh, oh, oh." Wren lay back with her hands behind her head. "A goblin of my very own. Just what I've always wanted. What do we do with him?"

I flopped down too, watching a distant black bird circling. A raven, I thought, but as it dropped lower and lower, almost as though it were trying to hear what we were saying, I changed my mind. A rook. You don't often see rooks in the mountains.

"If we let him go, he'll just follow us," I pointed out. I wondered who else was following us, and if she was using rooks to spy for her. I gave the bird a cheerful wave, just in case. It shot away out of sight at once.

Wren sat up, taking a twist of copper wire and her pliers out of her pocket. In a moment her hands were busy, bending and knotting the wire, reaching up to her hat to pluck out a pale brown feather, nipping off a few stalks of dull-green heather and working those in too. I watched, eager to see what the fancy was going to turn into. A faint, honey-colored light swelled and faded away again. But after another moment Wren sighed and put it back in her pocket.

"I don't like the idea of knowing there's a goblin somewhere behind us. I'd rather have him where I can see him."

"Me too," I agreed. "But he's going to be a real pain to travel with."

He was. The goblin fussed. He whined. He sulked and pouted. The sun was too bright and his head was woozy and his eyes hurt—well that was probably true, since goblins don't like the daylight much. But even after Wren made him a shady hat out of ferns, the complaints didn't stop. He was tired. His feet hurt. He was bored. The trees were boring. We were boring. He was hungry. He was thirsty. He needed to visit the bushes. Again. The sun was too hot. The wind was too cold. Ash was looking at him funny.

Still, Thimble really behaved himself quite well—for a goblin—as the trail led down to where the Wild Forest surged up against the mountains and we turned east under the eaves of the woods.

The goblins had left a horrible scar with their trampling and smashing. Even so, it was good to be in my own land again, though I hadn't been away for more than a few months. Wren strode along briskly, swinging her staff and singing.

"The gray geese are swiftly flying, And the autumn colors dying, And the clouds pile up to cover all the sky. But the fire's burning brightly, And the fiddle's dancing lightly…"

I joined in the last line. I was getting to know all of Wren's favorite songs by then. "And if you don't mind the weather, why should I?"

But…something bothered me, prickling like a spider crawling on my fur. Something was wrong with the Forest. My forest.

"Wren!" I called urgently. "Wait!"

"What?" she asked, looking around, staff ready, as if she expected another griffin attack.

"I'm not sure." I listened. I sniffed. There was a smell… something sick and rotten, something unnatural.

Wren sniffed too, but she obviously didn't smell anything.

"What are you looking for?" she asked. "Something dead?"

"Not exactly. Look there." I had found the source of the smell. I pointed to a young oak tree. Several of its lower branches had been twisted and broken by the goblins, but that wasn't what I wanted her to see.

"There's something cut in the bark," she said. "Some sort of symbol?" She went closer, and I beckoned Ash over, climbing onto his back so I could see better.

Wren frowned. "It's hard to see in all this flickering leaf-shadow, but just for a moment, I thought there was light, running along the lines."

I certainly didn't see that. "What kind of light?" I asked.

"A mucky red," she said. "Whatever this is, it makes my stomach feel kind of strange."

"It's sorcery," I said. "And it's a spell meant to do something nasty. It's full of ill-will, someone wishing very powerfully for something bad to happen." The symbol looked like a fancy knot, twisted and turning in on itself, the sort of knot you'd never get untied.

Knots like that you have to cut. But what was it meant to do? And why did I feel so dizzy, and the Forest look so odd, so dim and wavering, as if I was all of a sudden looking at it through restless water? There was a path opening up, almost a road, broad and inviting. Wren didn't see the shimmering forest, she told me later, just a broad, sunny green lane. She took a step towards it, as if she couldn't help herself. I grabbed her.

"No!" I said. "It's a trap!"

Bewilderment. People say "bewildered" when they mean confused, but it really means to lead someone astray, and it's also a powerful magic of the fairies, the Fair Folk of the Mounds. I wondered how a human sorcerer had learned such a spell. "He's made the Forest along here all folded up and twisted and tangled," I told Wren. "Like a knot with no beginning or end.

Or a labyrinth—a maze—only once you're inside there's no way out."

I felt a deep, hard anger begin to grow in my chest, a rage so deep the Forest felt it. How *dared* a human sorcerer, a kidnapper and goblin-friend, cast such spells on my Wild Forest? Wren gave me a worried look. Then she shivered. "It's getting dark and cold all of a sudden. Is there going to be a storm?"

I took a deep, calming breath. "No," I said. "It's just a passing cloud."

The Forest grew warm and bright again, and Wren looked back at the scarred tree. "So that's what happened to the knights?"

"The knights were lured into it and trapped," I agreed. "And they've probably been wandering ever since. They could wander for the rest of their lives and never find a path out, the way it's folded up on itself now." I could feel the tangle reaching ahead of us along the goblins' trail for miles and miles.

Wren pulled out her knife. "I'm going to cut that mark out of the tree. That should help."

"Yes," I agreed. But it wasn't going to end the spell, not all on its own. As Wren stood on tiptoe to slice away the bark with the symbol on it, I did something myself. It wasn't sorcery. I don't need sorcery. I just *wished*, and gave the Forest a sort of a shake and flick with my will, as you might shake the wrinkles out of a bedsheet. That straightened it. For a while.

"But a powerful spell like that isn't going to be anchored at only one point," I said aloud. "There will be more. This stretch of the Forest will be pulled crooked again unless we can find and destroy most of them."

Wren nodded, looking serious. "I've never seen you get angry before, Torrie," she said after a moment.

I shrugged and changed the subject. "We need to do something about that." I pointed at the sheet of bark in her hand. Wren was holding it as though it were poison ivy.

"How?" she asked. "Will I just ripping it up destroy the spell, or does it need something more?"

Her instincts were right. It needed something more. "We can burn it," I said. "Or throw it in swift running water. Either one should destroy its power."

"Fire," said Wren. "Because you look like you need a hot drink."

Over the following days we kept walking along the goblins' trail, and Wren, who had a sharp eye and was taller than me, found other symbols cut into trees, and charms made of woven twigs. They were all part of the same spell. I could feel the sorcery trying to twist the Forest up again, and I could feel the spell growing weaker with every charm and symbol that Wren destroyed. I hoped that would let the knights finally escape from wherever the road-illusion had taken them. However, we didn't see any sign of them until about two weeks after we had left the mountains.

At first we didn't realize that we *had* found a clue to the fate of the Twenty-Seven Royal Knights. We simply followed the goblins' trail, as we had been doing for so long, where it dipped down into a valley like a rounded bowl. A shallow stream poured over a low ledge, frothing into a deep, dark pool, from which it wound away between banks overhung with buttercups and forget-me-nots. At the far end of the valley, the stream dropped away in another waterfall. Between the two, the valley was an airy, open woodland of slender white birches, with ferns thick around their feet.

At least, it should have been.

Many of the trees had been hacked down. Smaller saplings were twisted and broken. On the southern side of the brook, most of the valley was black and burnt, stark bare trunks like sticks of charcoal rising from drifts of ashes. It stank of smoke.

"This was done only a day or so ago," I said. "The trail we've been following is a month old now, but this…"

Wren held her quarterstaff crossways in both hands, looking around, alert for goblins.

Only Thimble went pattering on ahead, uncaring. Ash snorted and tried to back away.

"Why didn't we smell the fire?" Wren asked.

"The wind was from the west. It was blowing from us towards the valley."

"Ah." Swinging her staff down to be a walking stick again, she gave my shoulder a squeeze. "Come on, Torrie. You can't do anything about it now, and we'd better investigate."

I nodded.

"Hurry up!" called Thimble, who had scrambled down into the valley. He was gathering an armful of charred branches. "Suppertime!"

A few hops and leaps and a bit of a slide took us down the short drop into the valley. As we drew near the goblin, he was trying to pull a branch off the biggest, oldest of the birches, despite all the broken, dead wood around him. This tree grew right on the north bank of the brook and had survived the fire. Its trunk divided into two forks; one had been chopped down and the other was hacked and hewn, but still alive. When one hand wasn't enough to pull a branch off the living trunk, Thimble dropped his armload of firewood and swung from that branch, bouncing up and down in his effort to break it.

The next minute he went flying, landing on his face in the ferns, and a wiry black root whipped free of the earth and stitched him to the ground.

CHAPTER SEVEN

In which Thimble is rescued

I never thought I'd find myself having to rescue a goblin. I have to admit that for a moment, as we stared at Thimble, flat on the ground with more and more snaky tree roots slithering over him, pulling him into the earth as he screeched and twitched and wailed, I thought, *serves him right*. Still, I don't like to see any creature suffering needlessly, and I thought Thimble might come in handy once we'd found the goblins' den. Even if he did have no sense of direction and couldn't have tracked a herd of elephants through fresh snow, he was bound to know the land around his own home—all the ways in and the good places to hide, that sort of thing.

Wren had already started running towards him. I overtook her.

"Stop that!" I shouted. "I know he's a goblin and you're probably not very happy with goblins right now, but we need him."

The roots stopped moving, but they didn't release their grip on Thimble. He was half-buried in the mud, and, though he had given up wailing, his eyes were popping and desperate, fixed pleadingly on us.

"Are you talking to the tree?" Wren asked, sounding a bit worried as she caught up. I don't know why, since if a tree could try to choke and bury a goblin, surely it could listen when someone shouted at it. But actually, I wasn't talking to the tree at all. Trees don't just up and decide to throttle people or bury them on their own.

Not birch trees, anyway. I've heard some willows can be quite nasty.

"I'm talking to the dryad," I said. "Can you see her, Wren?"

Dryads, as you probably know, are tree-spirits. They live in trees—not every tree, but in especially old trees, or trees that are unusually beautiful, or solitary, or twisty and interesting-looking. Some dryads live in groups, and some live all alone in a whole grove. This was the dryad of the entire valley of birches.

Wren shaded her eyes and squinted at the big birch tree.

"Um . . . " she said. "Maybe. There's a funny shimmer."

"That's her," I said. I gave the birch tree a little bow, to be polite. "Would you mind letting my friend see you?" I asked. "We need to talk, and you know how humans find it difficult to talk to things that aren't there."

"That is the human's problem, not mine," the dryad said, but she did let the girl see her, because Wren suddenly gasped, and then to my surprise she curtsied, which is tricky to do, especially if you're wearing trousers. "Madam!"

Yes, the dryad looked like someone who ought to be addressed as "Madam." She was very tall and slender, more or less human in shape (although I've never met a twelve-foot-tall human). Her skin was chalk white, like birchbark, and her eyes and hair were a shiny reddish-black, like birch twigs. She wasn't wearing anything at all; like me, dryads feel that clothes are a human thing. This is naturally very embarrassing for the humans they meet.

Well, actually she was wearing a wreath of flowers, but that probably doesn't count. Her long hair fell past her waist and stirred and fluttered in the wind.

"Torrie." The birch dryad gave me a solemn bow in return. She knew me, of course. Most other Old Things that belong to the Wild Forest do.

"Why are you speaking out for the goblin?" the dryad asked. She gave Wren a considering look. "And why are you traveling with this human?" She said the word "human" in pretty much the same tone of voice she had used for "goblin", the tone of voice that would go well with phrases like "this nasty, oozy slug."

"I often travel with humans," I said. "And I'm afraid the goblin is our prisoner, which makes us responsible for looking after him."

The dryad looked down at Thimble, and for a moment I was afraid she was going to lift one large, elegant foot, and squash him like a particularly uninteresting bug.

"He seems to be my prisoner now," she said.

Thimble moaned and tried to say something. It sounded like "Ee dur doot," but I think it was probably, "I didn't do it."

"What happened here?" Wren asked hastily, to distract the dryad.

"Goblins," the dryad hissed, her voice like a winter wind in bare branches. "And a sorcerer. He brought the goblins here. He told them to do their worst."

"Why?" I asked, shocked that a sorcerer would do such a thing. Even extremely wicked sorcerers usually have some respect for us OldThings.

Wren asked, "Was there a boy with them, a prisoner?"

"There was no boy." The dryad answered Wren first. "Just the sorcerer, and about a dozen goblins."

"But surely you could have stopped a dozen goblins," I said.

The dryad trembled in indignation, and her lovely dark eyes burned. She bent, swift as a supple birch lashing in a storm, and hauled Thimble up by the scruff of his neck, dangling him in the air and swinging him a little.

Thimble turned the color of cheese-wax and shut his eyes, curling into a ball.

"Please, madam," said Wren. "We really do need the goblin. We're following that sorcerer, to rescue the Crown Prince of High Morroway, and the goblin's going to help us. Aren't you, Thimble?" she added menacingly, twirling her staff in a casual way.

"Mm," Thimble grunted, still with his eyes shut.

"Goblins are no help to anyone, and you'll be a fool if you trust him," said the dryad. "And he stinks." She tossed Thimble into the stream.

He screamed and wailed and splashed like he was drowning,

but it was only a few feet deep, and he floundered out to the bank eventually.

"Hm," the dryad said then, watching Thimble scuttle away to cower among the burned stumps on the south side of the little valley. "Perhaps it doesn't work on goblins." She eyed Wren thoughtfully and gestured towards the brook. "Perhaps you'd like a drink, young goblin-friend?"

"Er, no, thank you," Wren said politely, backing away from the dryad. She gave the water a worried look, and raised her eyebrows at me.

I looked at the brook and shrugged. There didn't seem to me to be anything odd about it. I squatted down on the bank and dabbled my fingers in it.

"What's wrong with it?" I asked. I licked a drop off my fingers. The water tasted fine to me—cold and clean.

"Obviously nothing." The dryad sounded disappointed. She took one long stride into the water and stood there, with the current coiling and burbling around her. She sighed, and her hair curled and twisted as though she was taking up new life from the water.

"What was wrong with it?" Wren asked sternly, clearly getting over her awe of the dryad. "What did you think it was going to do?"

"I shouldn't have gotten involved," said the dryad. She plucked a handful of fresh buttercups and begin tucking them into her hair. "It wasn't any of my business. They were just humans. I should have kept my mouth shut."

"Who were just humans?" Wren asked.

"Nobody's *just* humans," I said. "And being angry at the sorcerer is no reason to try to trick Wren into doing something dangerous, simply because she didn't want you squashing Thimble."

"Mm." The dryad did not look entirely convinced. "You keep that goblin of yours from pointlessly killing trees, young human, or I shan't bother with any tricking, next time."

"He's not my goblin," Wren retorted. "But yes, while he's with us we'll try to make him behave. Now tell us what's wrong with the water."

"It started quite a while ago, before the snow had hardly melted," the dryad said. She waded gracefully across the brook and began to pace slowly back and forth along the other bank, where everything was burnt and black. I could feel, as she walked, the roots of the charred ferns and the flowers and even some of the stumps that weren't entirely dead beginning to tingle with stronger life, stretching hungrily through the dark earth.

I knew the beginning of a story when I heard one, so I sat down on the ground and made myself comfortable. After a moment, Wren did the same, though she took care not to sit under any of the few lively looking trees, and she kept her staff close to hand.

"The sorcerer came here, riding up from the east on his white horse one night. He was leading a band of goblins. I was slow and sleepy then, only starting to wake." The dryad shuddered, the way you might have seen a horse shudder a fly off its hide. "They went trampling through with their horrid, crushing feet. But they didn't stay, they kept on going, and I forgot about them. Then, a month ago, they came back, marching through again one evening. I turned the trees against them. They tripped on the roots and were lashed by branches and a few had dead branches drop on their heads. Pity goblins have such hard heads. But that hurried them on their way. I didn't think they'd be back."

"But they were," Wren said, her voice gentle with sympathy.

"Yesterday. . ." The dryad tossed her head angrily, and a sharp little breeze whirled around the valley. "Early yesterday morning the sorcerer came back again, with a dozen goblins. He rode into the valley bold as you please and started striding about, poking into things and talking to himself. I told him to leave and he *ignored* me."

"Could he see you?" asked Wren.

"I made very certain he could." The dryad sounded insulted, as well as angry. "And then he said that I should be quiet and not bother him, since he was working on a complicated spell. In *my valley*, mind you."

"What about the goblins?" I asked.

"Oh, they were all huddled together by the lower waterfall, watching. They were afraid of me, but they were all sniggering and giggling, too."

"Did you try to stop the sorcerer?" I asked. "Is that why?" And I waved a hand around the valley.

"No," the dryad said. "I wanted to know what he was up to. I followed him. He went up and down the brook, picking up stones from the water and tying things to them and whispering over them before he threw them back."

"What sort of things?" Wren asked, giving the brook a suspicious look.

"Bones, mostly," the dryad said. "Tiny, white bones."

Wren made a face.

"I had had enough. I was about to take him by the scruff of the neck and throw him out of the valley when I heard a sound. Horses, jingling and thudding, in the forest west of the valley. The sorcerer jumped on his own horse and went tearing down past the lower falls, with the goblins after him, and in a moment a horse and rider appeared on the path by the upper falls."

"A knight," Wren guessed. "A Royal Knight of Morroway."

"A human knight," the dryad agreed. "It looked very tired, very tattered and battered, and so did the horse. They came clomping down, tearing up the bank almost as badly as the goblins had, and behind them came another, and another. A whole herd of knights and horses, and the knights had mailshirts and iron helmets." The dryad wrapped her arms about herself, as if she were cold. "Iron horseshoes," she said. "Treading all over the roots of my trees. It made me ill."

"It would," I said sympathetically. A dryad, of course, is very connected to her trees.

"They all staggered to a stop and looked around, blinking and staring, as if they were coming out of a fog. Most of them got down and helped the ones that seemed to be too tired. They didn't unharness their horses, but they let them drink, and brushed off the worst of the mud, and the poor creatures started grazing as if they hadn't eaten for a month. And the knights drank themselves, of course."

"But the sorcerer…" "Wren and I said together.

"I tried to warn them then," the dryad said. "I let them hear me and see me, and I called out *Beware the water!* when the first one went to dip up a drink in his hands. And they looked all around and one of them said, *Now he's going to try to stop us drinking.* And another said to me, *Are you a fairy? Are you in league with the sorcerer?* I said, *The sorcerer has bespelled the water.* So that one asked, *To do what?* I had to tell her I didn't know. So she told the others, *The horses drank, and nothing happened to them. Let me drink and test it. I'm the youngest and the least loss if something bad happens.* And before they could stop her she plunged her face in and drank."

"What happened?" Wren and I asked in the same breath.

"Nothing," said the dryad. "They waited, and still nothing happened. They looked at me, and said, *We know that it was a sorcerer who took the prince. First a landslide out of nowhere, and an ambush by griffins, and then the Forest turning into a nightmare. Only a sorcerer could have trapped us like that. Where is she?* So I told them, *Just down the hill there.* And they laughed. They didn't believe me. And they all drank."

"And?"

"And then the woman who had drunk first fell down and disappeared, and only her armor and clothing were left in a heap on the ground."

"The water melted her?" Wren cried in horror.

"No," said the dryad. "It would have been quite funny, really, if it hadn't been so terrible. They all shouted and ran over, drawing their swords, as if that would help. And they pulled apart the heap of clothes—look."

She pointed. Wren and I looked. What had seemed to be an ashy rock was actually a jumble of clothes and armor, with a single boot still standing upright.

"What happened?" I asked impatiently.

"A toad jumped away," the dryad said.

Wren stared. "A toad?"

"And then it started happening to the others."

I looked around. Now that I knew what I was looking for, I could see that were at least a couple dozen of those forlorn heaps of clothing, but ashes and cinders from the fire had drifted over them, making me mistake them for rocks and burned stumps. Some of the heaps, the ones on the south side of the valley, were burnt, and only the blackened armor and buckles were left.

"Were the toads caught in the fire?" I asked softly, almost afraid to hear the answer.

"The sorcerer and the goblins came back," the dryad said. "He had the goblins catch all the toads and put them in a sack. And then he told them…" her eyes snapped like coals on the hearth, flaring red in their dark depths, "…he told them, *Show her what happens to people who try to foil Lord Abastor's revenge. It looks like a good place for a bonfire, doesn't it? Go ahead and do your worst.* They had axes, iron axes, and they hacked and they slashed and they burned—even though it was broad daylight—and they ran around whooping and yelling. They didn't bother with a bonfire, they just set fires all over. I tried to stop them. I threw the first two of them who raised an axe down over the waterfall. But the sorcerer chanted something and froze me. Trapped me helpless in my tree as if I were a mere child, a sapling, and all I could do was watch."

"It's no wonder you wanted to kill Thimble," Wren said. "And I'm really very sorry. I can see this was a beautiful place."

"And it will be again," I said firmly. "It isn't dead. Life will come back."

"But not for years." The dryad wept, hiding her face in her hair.

I waded across the stream, not without a little shiver of worry, I admit, but nothing happened. I patted the dryad comfortingly on her knee. "No," I admitted. "It won't be the way it was, not for years. But it will come back, so long as you're here, the heart of the grove."

"And we're going to rescue Prince Liasis," said Wren. "Helping us will be your revenge on this Lord Abastor."

"Kill him," said the dryad savagely, looking up.

"I'm not promising that," Wren said. "But I'll do what I can to see he's punished." She got to her feet again. "From what you say, madam, we're not very far behind the sorcerer at all now, so we should really get going. Thank you for telling us what happened to the knights. And for not squashing Thimble."

The dryad frowned over at the goblin, who was beating a broken branch on the charred trunk of a tree, trying to break it. "If I ever see him again, he will be squashed," she said. Giving me a bow and a faint smile, she strode to her tree again and faded into it.

"Well," said Wren. She gave the brook a wistful look. "I'm awfully thirsty. Just knowing I can't drink the water is making me need to."

"It's probably fine," I said. "There's something about running water that makes it very hard to enchant. By now, the transformation spell is bound to have all washed away, even if those charms haven't."

"Would the charms have been made from toad bones?" Wren asked.

"Very likely," I said.

Wren looked thoughtful. "Scales," she said to herself. "Hm." But then she eyed me, standing on the edge of the brook. "Do you really think it's safe?"

"Yes."

"You try the water, then," she said.

"I already did," I pointed out. "Ribbid."

"That's frogs. And what if it only works on humans?"

"Do something for me," I told her. "Sort of half close your eyes, and relax. Just look at the water, and lose yourself in it."

"You think I might see something, like in the forest?"

"Try it. What do you see?"

"The brook," she said, her eyes half closed. "You know, water and stones and flowers, and I think there's a big trout or some-thing hiding in the shadow under the bank."

"Fine," I said. "Now do the same thing and look at the dryad's tree."

Wren sighed dramatically, but she turned her gaze to the old birch.

"Now what do you see?"

"Huh!" She gave a grunt of surprise. "It's almost…outlined. A silvery glow, like when the moon's behind a thick cloud with the light just catching the edge of it. It's beautiful."

"Hm," I said. "Right. I think the water's probably safe to drink."

"So," Wren said slowly. "Torrie, can anyone see sorcery, then, if they know how to look? Or is it something you're helping me to do?"

"It's nothing to do with me," I said. "Really, it's too bad you don't know a little about your family."

"Why?"

"Well, it would be interesting to know if any of your relatives were sorcerers."

Wren shrugged. "I suppose. Do you have to have relatives that do magic, to see magic?"

"No," I said. "But it often does run in families, like having curly hair or something. It doesn't mean you will. It doesn't mean you won't. It just makes it more likely."

"I suppose being able to see sorcery could come in handy," said Wren thoughtfully. "At least in this adventure. Not much use for everyday things, though."

"You never know," I said. "And magic isn't something that some people can only see. Sometimes you'll notice it with your other senses. The brook doesn't smell funny or sound peculiar to you either, does it?"

Wren took a deep breath and scooped up a handful of water, sniffing it.

"Smells like water," she said. She lapped at it with her tongue, like a suspicious cat. "Tastes like water."

"Yipes!" I yelled.

Wren flung the water away and stumbled back. "What?"

"I thought—just for a moment there—I thought you were growing a wart on the end of your nose."

Wren picked me up and dumped me in the brook. I shrieked—it was very cold—and grabbed her around the knees, hauling her in after me. We yelped and laughed and tried to duck one another.

Thimble came scampering over. "Are you drowning?" he asked helpfully. "If you drown, I can have your cheeses, right?"

But we were both laughing too hard to answer him.

Just above the lower waterfall we waded out, pleasantly cool and dripping. Wren sat on the bank to dump out her sloshing boots, and looked around.

"Where's Ash got to?"

She whistled. After a moment there was a jingle of harness and a rustle of bushes. Ash's nose poked out of a thicket of birch saplings that had escaped the tree-slaughter.

"Don't eat the trees," said Wren hastily. "We've had a hard enough time convincing the dryad to let Thimble go as it is."

"Why did you bother?" asked Ash, but I didn't translate that. "Look what I've found, Torrie." He trotted across the crunching, burned ground to us. "Am I clever, or what? I bet these lads can tell you all about what happened to the Knights."

"We already know," I started to say, but I was interrupted by an indignant, horsy voice.

"Lads and lasses!" Another horse, tall, black, and strong, shouldered her way out of the thicket behind Ash.

There were two stallions behind her, one a pale gold color and one brown and white spotted. The three of them stood in a row behind Ash, looking at us suspiciously, their nostrils flaring.

"The rest are down in the forest," the pony said. "They don't like the smell of the fire up here."

"Warhorses," said Wren.

"A goblin!" said the black mare, and she shoved Ash neatly out of the way with her shoulder and charged at us, head low, teeth bared. The other two were right behind her. Ash squealed and bolted away. Wren grabbed an overhanging branch and heaved herself up into a half-burned tree. I scrambled up another, trying to drag Thimble with me, but he struggled free and instead dropped to the ground, covering his head. I think I've mentioned that goblins generally aren't very bright?

"No! No! No!" I shouted. "We've already gone through this with the dryad! Don't hurt the goblin, we need him to rescue the prince."

The black mare came to a thundering, snorting halt. Another few strides and Thimble would have been minced to dog's meat.

"*You're* rescuing the prince?" The pale gold stallion's tone was not very flattering.

Wren and I got down from our trees, and Wren pulled Thimble up by the scruff of the neck, giving him a shake.

"I really don't understand how anyone ever let you out on your own," she said. "Torrie, what are we going to do with twenty-seven horses?"

In which Liasis meets some toads, and Bobbin loses a treasure

"It's all right, really," Liasis hissed, his tongue flickering worriedly. "I'm not going to eat you, I promise."

An eye like an amber jewel peered at him from beneath a dead oak leaf and then disappeared. Leaves rustled as the toad shuffled backwards, further from sight.

"Sir Eglantine, Sir Rufous, please. All of you, come out. I *promise*."

"It's easy to promise," said a rough, toady sort of voice from deep under the leaves. "But you're a snake. We feel it in our bones: you eat toads. So you probably feel it too, Your Highness. *Ah, toads, dinner,* that's what your bones are thinking, no matter what you know in your head."

"But Sir Rufous——"

"I'm Eglantine," the toad said, sounding a bit annoyed. Eglantine was the prince's best friend among the Royal Knights.

She was the youngest of them, not that many years older than Liasis, and he had always thought she was quite pretty, with her long coppery pigtails, although wild horses couldn't have made him admit it.

I've always wondered why people say that. I mean, I've met a few wild horses in my time, and I've never noticed that they're that keen on getting people to confess to deep, dark secrets.

"Sorry, Eglantine," said Liasis.

"I'm Rufous," said another toady voice, from even deeper under the leaves. Rufous was Eglantine's older brother.

"You see, Your Highness?" said the first toad. Liasis thought that one was probably Sir Acer, the King's Champion, or maybe his wife, Sir Salix. "You can't even tell us apart. We probably all look like dinner."

"None of you look like dinner," Liasis said desperately. "I give you my word, I won't eat you." He tried to make his voice sound princely and commanding. "Now stop being foolish and come out where I can see you. Where have you been? Have you been toads all this time?"

"All what time?" one of them asked.

"Actually, that's a good question," said another. "I thought, there in that little dell, that things didn't look quite right. That rowan tree by the waterfall as we came down had green berries on it. But the rowans were in flower when we rode into the Wild Forest."

The toads were silent.

"I'm not sure of the exact date," Liasis said, "but I think June is over."

"It was the middle of May when we left the mountains and rode into the Wild Forest," said a knight carefully. "Are you sure you haven't miscounted, Highness?"

"Not by that much. What happened to you all?" Liasis asked.

"We were careful! After that landslide, and those griffins that attacked us in the mountains, we were watching for ambushes!"

"Not well enough, obviously," a toad grumbled.

"There wasn't anything to notice. We kept following the goblin's trail down into the Wild Forest. And then, well, we all knew we were going the right way on this wide green lane, and we almost had them. But a fog came up as night fell."

Another toad took up the story. "We could hear…things."

"It was like a nightmare, when you know that just out of reach, just out of sight behind you, something's there. Something terrible."

"The trees leaned in, and the wind roared, but the fog didn't blow away."

"There were no stars. Between the gaps in the trees, it was all dark, blacker than a cloudy night."

"We couldn't make camp. We just rode to get out of it. Rode and rode."

"Obviously we didn't ride for six weeks," said a toad crisply. That was probably Sir Salix again. It was the kind of thing she would say. "Both we and the horses would have dropped dead of exhaustion long before then, even before we died of thirst and hunger."

"We rode for hours and hours, like in a dream that won't end."

"A nightmare."

"I already said that."

"And then everything seemed to shiver and shudder, and there was a light like dawn—a break in the fog."

"So we rode out and found ourselves in a different part of the Wild Forest, following the goblin trail down past a little waterfall and into a dell full of birch trees."

"Which is where we all had a drink and turned into toads."

"My poor Swallow," said Eglantine. "I hate to think what will happen to the horses."

"At least we're all together," said Liasis. "We need to have a...a council of war. We need to make plans."

"You listen to Prince Snaky," Bobbin advised from up above.

"The goblin's still here!" croaked a knight.

"Hush!"

"Shh!"

"Spying on us!"

"I'm not!" Bobbin cried out. "I'm just takin' an interest."

"You'd better go away for now, Bobbin," Liasis said apologetically. "After all, you are on Lord Abastor's side."

"I'm not," Bobbin grumbled. "Don't like him at all."

"He's still your goblin lord. And if you accidentally overheard us talking about how to escape or something, you'd tell him."

"Wouldn't! Anyway, there's no way you can escape from the Pit. Toads can't jump high, not like froggies. An' if you do make a cunning plan, I promise I won't tell. I could even help. I'm good at cunning plans."

"As if we'd believe a goblin could keep a secret," said Sir Rufous scornfully.

"I keep lots of secrets!" said Bobbin, leaning over the edge of the Pit and scowling.

"Yeah? Like what?" squeaked another toad.

"I told you, it wouldn't be secret, would it?" Bobbin hesitated. "I'll show you, if you promise not to tell."

"Show us what?" Liasis asked.

"Well, that's a secret," Bobbin said. "Promise?"

"All right, we promise," said Liasis. "Right?" When there was silence, he slithered a bit closer to the pile of leaves. "Promise her, Knights." He meant to sound princely and commanding again, but probably he just sounded like a snake that was thinking about twenty-seven dinners.

There were twenty-seven mumbled croakings of "Yes" and "I promise."

Bobbin perched on the lip of the Pit, dangling her feet over. "I haven't told even my brother Thimble about this secret, 'cause he's an idiot and a blabbermouth. But I'll tell you and then you'll let me help you make your cunning plans."

"We don't want you to help us," said the toad who was either Sir Acer or Sir Salix. "We don't care about your secret, you nasty, smelly, wicked little creature."

But Bobbin was already undoing the drawstring of the leather purse at her waist. She paused for a moment to cross her eyes and stick out her tongue. "You're a nasty rude slimy warty toad and I hope Prince Snaky does eat you, so there." She grinned at Liasis, showing all her teeth. "Shut your eyes."

"I can't," Liasis said, rather patiently, he thought.

"Ready?" Bobbin wasn't listening. "Now look!" She pulled

something sparkling out of her purse and dangled it over the Pit.

"Oh!" said a toad that Liasis was fairly sure was Eglantine.

What Bobbin was dangling over his head was a necklace. Small discs of milky blue turquoise, each clasped in a delicate frame of gold, were strung together on a golden chain.

"Beautiful!" said another toad.

"Where did you steal it from?" asked Sir Acer sternly.

"Didn't!" said Bobbin, and stuck out her tongue again. "Found it! Thimble and me were exploring—"

"Thimble and *I* were exploring," corrected a toad, in a way that made Liasis certain she was Sir Salix.

"You don't even know Thimble," said Bobbin. "Do you? So why were you exploring with him?"

"I wasn't exploring with Thimble!" protested Sir Salix.

"You just said you were."

"I didn't."

"Did too."

"I was correcting your grammar."

"Well don't. I never liked my grammar, or my gramper neither, but it's not up to some silly toady knight to go correcting them." Bobbin swung the necklace back and forth. "Anyhow, I didn't steal this, and neither did my grammar, though she stole lots of good stuff in her day. I found it when Thimble and me or you was exploring this old ruined city way off up in the mountains, before Snip and Snag ever led us down here to this swamp. It was stuck in a crack between the stones, all muddy and covered in ick. Probably it'd been there ever since some violet-eating princessy type lost it a hundred years ago, and I found it, not Thimble. He found starling's eggs to eat and didn't share, so I kept this and didn't share. So see, I know all about secrets and if you're going to have a secret plot, you have to tell me or I won't bring you any nice fresh earthworms, only old stale squashed ones. So *nyah!*"

"What have you got there, Shuttle?" asked a deep, human voice. "You're supposed to be guarding the snake, not teasing it."

Bobbin squeaked and her gray face went an even uglier milky yellow color. She started frantically stuffing the necklace back into her purse, but Lord Abastor crouched down behind her, gripped her firmly by the ear and plucked the jewels from her hands.

"Hm," he said. "Didn't I say that all plunder was to be given to me, so that it could be shared out fairly?"

"It's not plunder, my lord," Bobbin whined. "It's mine. I found it, a long time ago."

"Not a very likely story," Lord Abastor said. He held the necklace up, looking at it in the light from that small crack in the roof.

Abastor's fingers touched the turquoise discs gently. "Her eyes were just this color," he said softly, and for a moment his face looked sad and dreamy, even handsome. Then it became sharp and hard again. "This is too precious a thing to leave in the hands of a careless goblin," he said. "You can have an extra ration of stew at supper, Treadle, since you're the one who found it. But it belongs to the whole goblin band, not just to you, and as your lord I shall look after it and keep it safe."

"But it's mine!" Bobbin wailed, as the necklace disappeared into Lord Abastor's pocket.

"Don't be greedy," he said sternly, standing up. "You, Prince Liasis—still enjoying your new shape?"

"No, not really," Liasis said, hoping he sounded more bold and defiant than he felt.

"A pity. You'd better get used to it. I have no intention of changing you back. And how are the toads settling in? I just came down to let you know you won't be here much longer. You and the knights . . . Thimble, what happened to those toads? I told you not to eat them."

"Hmph," was all Bobbin said.

"They're hiding," said Liasis, not wanting Bobbin to get into any more trouble. She seemed to be the only chance he had of a friend in this place. "

"Ah, brave knights. Well, Your Highness, you and the knights should learn to enjoy your new forms, since, as I said, you'll be spending the rest of your lives in them. I'm going to give you to the sultan's menagerie in Callipepla. You'll be safe from being eaten by other animals if you're in the zoo. I did promise you wouldn't be hurt, after all. And they have a very nice reptile house. "

"Toads," said Liasis coldly, "are amphibians."

Abastor waved a dismissive hand. "Reptiles, amphibians, creepy crawlies. I had more important things to study when I was a boy." He turned to leave.

"Wait!" croaked a toad commandingly. "Whom did you promise that you wouldn't hurt us?"

"He won't answer that," said Liasis. "I've already tried. But Lord Abastor, please. There's nothing we can do. We're

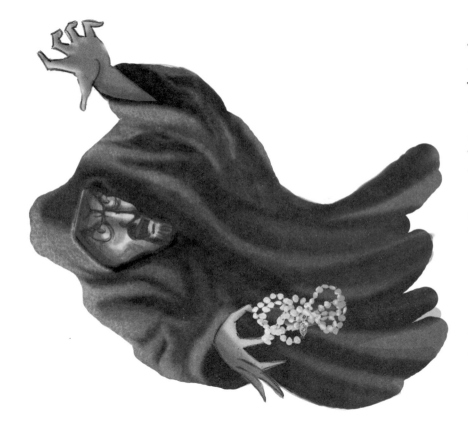

completely in your power." Or was he being too obvious?

"So please, tell us. Why are you sending us to the zoo? I mean, didn't you kidnap me for ransom or something?"

"No," said Abastor. "I didn't. Do I look like some poverty-stricken second-rate enchanter who has to blackmail people into giving me money? My mother was a princess of Callipepla, and the sultan is a distant relative. I certainly don't need money and, if I did, I wouldn't try to get it from a poor little kingdom like yours." He snickered. "What could I hold you hostage for? Cheese curds? Buttermilk?"

"But this doesn't make any sense," Liasis protested. "You don't just kidnap people and turn them into things for no reason."

"Don't you tell me what I do and do not do, Your Highness," snapped Abastor. "I do what I want to do, when I want to do it, and there's nobody who can stop me."

"You said something about revenge to that fairy in the dell," a toad said.

"She was a dryad, you ignorant human," Abastor sneered. "And what if I did?"

"That's really very childish," said Eglantine quietly, her voice muffled beneath the leaves.

"That's childish," said Liasis, more loudly, because he was so angry he didn't care what Abastor did. "And anyway, revenge for what? What's High Morroway ever done to you? Did you buy a bad cheese or something?"

Abastor stared down at him. "Ah. That was meant to be sarcastic humor, was it? You know, I don't know what anybody could ever have seen in that oafish father of yours. And you certainly seem to take after him. I think that you can just go on guessing. It'll give you something to do to pass the time in the zoo." He spun on his heel and stalked off, his cloak billowing over the Pit as he turned.

"Stupid thieving stuck-up sorcerer!" screamed Bobbin, when the sound of Abastor's boots had died away. "Stupid, stupid,

stupid cheating lying nose-in-the-air lord!" She bounded down into the Pit, landing on the drift of leaves. Toads scattered in all directions. "I'll show him! Those jewels are mine, mine, mine!"

She snatched Liasis up and vaulted out again. "I'll show him revenge!"

"Hey!" croaked Sir Acer. "You can't steal the prince!"

"What about us?" croaked Sir Eglantine. "Hey, goblin, take us too!"

Their voices died away as Bobbin scampered along a dark tunnel.

"Not so tight!" Liasis gasped, and the goblin loosened her hold on him a little. He took a grateful gasp of air. "Where are we going?"

"He steals my necklace, I'm going to steal his prince," said Bobbin. Her eyes gleamed red in the darkness. "No, even better, first I'm going to steal my necklace right back. And you're going to help, Snaky Prince, if you want to get home to your nice castle and feast on candied swans and roast violets ever again."

CHAPTER NINE

In which snakes can fly

"This is a very bad idea," Liasis said. "Look, why don't you just help me get home to High Morroway? You can explain what happened, my father can find a sorcerer to make me human again, and then we'll declare war on Lord Abastor and you'll get your necklace back."

"No," said Bobbin.

"At least we should wait until morning, when Abastor goes out."

"We've already been waiting all day. The sun's set, and he acts like a human and goes to bed at night. He'll be asleep now."

"But it's too dangerous. What if he wakes up?"

"You promised to help, and you got to keep your promises because you're a prince."

"That's not why. Everyone should keep their promises. And I don't remember . . ."

Oh. But he did. He'd told Bobbin, "If there's ever anything I can do for you…" But he hadn't meant burgling a sorcerer's bedroom while the sorcerer was actually in bed. Anyone with any sense would have known that.

"You promised."

"All right, all right. I'll take a look." A very, very quick look. And since Abastor probably hadn't left the necklace lying on the floor where a snake could get it, he could truthfully tell Bobbin he didn't see it, and they could come up with a more sensible plan.

"Just don't get caught." Bobbin placed him carefully on the floor.

Liasis stretched and flickered his tongue. From down here, the gap under the door of Lord Abastor's private room looked like a fine entrance for a small garter snake, at least an inch high, maybe even an inch and a half. Liasis took a deep breath, summoning his courage, and slithered under the door.

The prince was expecting—almost anything. Bubbling alchemical experiments. Stacks of ancient books. Whirling brass devices, stuffed animals, strange skeletons. But this was just a bedroom, with a curtained bed, a sheepskin rug, an iron-bound chest that probably contained the goblin band's loot, and a little, low table by the bed, on which he could just see the corner of a book and a tall gold candlestick.

So Lord Abastor, like Liasis, enjoyed reading in bed at night. The beeswax candle was burning brightly. Obviously no one had ever scolded the enchanter about how dangerous it was to go to sleep leaving a candle burning. Perhaps, Liasis thought sourly, the bed-curtains would catch fire and solve all his problems. Or if Abastor died, would the spell last forever?

A fire burned on the hearth, flinging a pleasant heat out into the room. A window was cut into one stone wall, an arched hole without any glass, and in the far corner of the room there was a folding wooden screen. A threadbare red robe hung over it.

No turquoise necklace. Liasis was tempted to linger near the fire to warm his cold blood, but at any moment Abastor might wake up and remember the candle. The flame danced in the breeze from the window, and something else on the stand by the bed caught the prince's eye. It almost looked like...but it couldn't be.

Nevertheless, he slithered nearer. The little table wasn't a fine piece of furniture. In fact, it looked like it could have been made by the goblins themselves. The top was just a slice out of a tree and the legs, which weren't all quite the same height, were slender stems from young spruces, with the rough bark still on them. Liasis swarmed up quite easily, though his weight made the table rock with a quiet *tock* on the floor. He froze, but nothing stirred beyond the drawn bedcurtains.

And what he had glimpsed from the floor was true after all. He couldn't believe it. He was nose to nose with a painting of a face he knew well.

His stepmother, Demansia.

She looked out at him from a small oval frame. The portrait made her look very young, hardly more than a girl. She smiled shyly, and her black hair was loose, flowing down over her shoulders. Her gown was just the color of her eyes, sky blue with a hint of green.

Just the color of turquoise, Liasis realized. Just the color of the stones in the lumpy, cold heap he was lying on—Bobbin's necklace.

He remembered, now, Queen Demansia saying there was another man who had wanted to marry her, a distant relative of the sultan himself. She had said no, because she was in love with King Boiga of High Morroway, whom she had met when he made a state visit to the sultan of Callipepla. Also, she had found the other man a little scary, although she had not explained why.

And Abastor had talked about revenge. Now Liasis understood. He wasn't kidnapped for ransom, but to make his father and Demansia miserable.

Liasis had studied enough history to know that when the heir to the crown disappears, usually there's some villain behind it, a villain close to him. An ambitious aunt or uncle, a wicked stepmother…and someone had helped Abastor, he couldn't forget that. But he knew it could never have been Demansia. He had to get to back to High Morroway, before the kingdom was ruined by mistrust and suspicion. People might even start taking sides and fighting. Maybe that was part of what Abastor planned; Bobbin had said something about him telling the goblins they would be allowed to have the whole kingdom to pillage and plunder, and a kingdom in chaos would certainly be easier for goblins to raid. For a moment Liasis wanted nothing so much as to be within biting distance of Lord Abastor. He didn't even wish to be human again; he just wanted to hurt the sorcerer, right there and then.

There was a clang, a bit like someone banging their elbow on the side of a tin bathtub. And a splash. The sounds came from behind the wooden screen in the corner.

Liasis's heart beat so quickly he could feel it pounding against his delicate snake ribs.

A hiss made him look around. Bobbin had pushed the door ajar and was peering in.

"Psst! Prince Snaky! You found it yet?" she whispered. "Hurry up."

Someone yawned, loudly, as if just waking up after falling asleep in the bath. And water sloshed and splashed again.

Bobbin's mouth fell open, her eyes wide.

Liasis whipped around, too quickly, and went clattering down to the stone floor in a heap with the candlestick and the portrait and the turquoise necklace. The candle went out.

"Who's there?" demanded a man's voice, and there was more splashing.

"Hah!" yelped Bobbin, and she dove into the room, sliding on her stomach along the floor to the gleaming tangle of the necklace. Liasis, racing towards the door as fast as he could go, ran into her.

"What!" roared the sorcerer. "*What* do you think you are doing, Thimble?"

"Bobbin!" screamed the goblin, bouncing to her feet with Liasis and the necklace clutched together in one hand. "My name's Bobbin, Bobbin, Bobbin! You stupid, stupid, stupid— *half-human!* What kind of an Old Thing are you, can't even tell us apart!"

Old Thing? Liasis wondered, even as he was choking. Half-human?

And as a dripping Lord Abastor stormed towards her, with the red robe wrapped crookedly around him, a wild blue flame dancing over one upraised hand, Bobbin kicked the sorcerer in the shin.

Abastor roared again and his blue flame winked out. He grabbed Bobbin by one big pointed ear, but Bobbin was too enraged to notice.

"What kind of goblin lord are you, can't even bother trying to remember our names!" She drew back her arm and, with a strong underhand toss, sent Liasis and the necklace flying out the window in one scaly, sparkling knot.

This time, Liasis knew he really was going to die.

But he didn't. He splashed. The weight of the necklace pulled him down through shallow water, until he and it were resting on soft mud. For a moment, Liasis was too stunned to do anything. Then he squirmed free of the golden chain and swam to the surface, poking his head out cautiously. He was in a narrow channel, about two feet wide and just as deep, which twisted and turned between hummocks of tall, broad-bladed grass. About thirty feet away, on a small island, a great mound of solid rock shone pale in the moonlight. It looked like a small stone hill that had begun to grow into a palace. It even had carved balconies. Firelight escaped from a few windows, including, closest to him, the window Bobbin had thrown him from—Lord Abastor's.

The sorcerer's voice echoed over the swamp. "You…you…you—!" He seemed at a loss for words.

Bobbin sobbed and screeched, but both her wails and Abastor's sputterings were getting fainter, as though he was dragging her off somewhere. Liasis almost felt sorry for the goblin.

No, he realized. He *was* sorry for her. She had set him free and been captured herself. But if he didn't want to be recaptured, he had to get away from Abastor's window, because the first thing the sorcerer would do, once he had done whatever he was going to do to Bobbin, would be to search for the necklace and his prisoner.

Liasis dove down into the mud and grabbed the necklace in his mouth. Towing its dragging weight, he started swimming along the channel. It twisted and turned and divided like a maze, moving out deeper and deeper into the swamp. When he came to a fallen willow, Liasis dove again and dropped the turquoise and gold chain down into the dark hollow beneath its roots. There. If Bobbin escaped and he ever saw her again, he could tell her where to find her treasure.

Then he swam again, farther and farther from the dark shape against the stars that was the goblins' island. He hadn't gone very far, though, before voices began to carry over the water. Goblins splashed and shouted and giggled and screeched. Torches popped and flared and made the damp night air taste like smoke and pine pitch. The calls of the night birds— the gronking of a nighthawk, the sad song of the whip-poor-will, the distant hwooo of an owl—fell silent.

"Locked up in the stable? What did she do?"

"Bit his lordship!"

"Kicked him!"

"Serves her right, she was trying to steal our loot."

"Ate that enchanted snake she was supposed to be guarding."

"Spied on his lordship in his bath."

That got a chorus of guffawing laughter.

"Found it! Found it!"

"That's just a root."

"Oh."

Liasis swam still farther, through cattails now, until he found a small, damp knoll, covered in pussywillows and wild cucumber, where he could crawl up out of the water and lie hidden for the night.

With the first pale dawn light the goblins, black from head to toe with muck from the bottom of the swamp, trudged and splashed back to their island den.

Lord Abastor was not going to be pleased, Liasis thought happily, watching them go through the waving greenery. Now he just had to find his way back to High Morroway and Morroway Castle, without being eaten by any of the things that ate garter snakes, and then somehow show people who he was. Maybe he could write his name in the dirt?

It would help if he knew where he was, of course, and more importantly, where High Morroway was. The rising sun was flooding the swamp with light. Poking his head farther out from the tangle of vines, he could see the snow-covered peaks of the mountains.

The mountains were in the wrong place. They were south, towering up higher than he had ever realized they could.

He just couldn't do it. Liasis couldn't see how a rather small garter snake could travel all through the mountains, looking for a kingdom that was also rather small, as kingdoms went. He had made it as far as the southern edge of what seemed to be an extremely large swamp by the time he realized that. He had also realized something else. It kept nagging and pricking at his mind, like a thorn in your foot you just can't ignore even when you try not to walk on it.

He couldn't abandon Bobbin, even if she was only a goblin. She was, well, maybe not his friend, exactly, but his ally. She had tried to help. And when she knew there was no escape for her, she had thrown him out the window to freedom. He owed her.

He headed back towards the goblins' island and passed another night hidden beneath a tangle of vines.

When the sun rose again, burning off the night mists and warming the sluggish blood of all the frogs and turtles and snakes of the swamp, it found Liasis on the goblins' island, slithering around the fortress.

The first entrance he found was an archway facing east. A pair of goblin guards slouched in the shade, keeping away from the bright light. Although the doorway looked fairly large to Liasis, it wasn't tall enough for a horse, so it couldn't be the stable. Anyway, he really didn't like the idea of crawling in past goblin feet and sharp axes. He kept going. He was almost halfway around the north side when he felt a stirring in the air above him. His snake instincts took over and he shot into the shelter of a tuft of grass. A huge, spearlike beak stabbed after him.

"Go away!" Liasis hissed. "I'm not a snake, I'm a human."

"Food," croaked the heron. "Good." Its eyes were glassy and glaring, and there wasn't any real thought behind them, just the need to eat. Liasis tried to burrow deeper into the plants, but the heron stalked after him, tearing away great clumps of grass.

Something else dropped out of sky, croaking and cawing, diving at the heron. Even though it was much larger, the heron

leapt back in alarm, flapping its great slate-blue wings, and then, trailing its legs, soared out over the water to look for fish instead. Liasis barely had time to heave a sigh of relief before a black shape stuck its head into the tuft of grass, a shiny green eye tilting this way and that. Then a black beak darted and this time Liasis just wasn't fast enough. He was dragged from his hiding place and the bird leapt into the air, swooping low over the goblin den with Liasis dangling from its beak. When he squirmed, it merely tightened its grip.

The raven or crow—or whatever it was—dropped lower and lower until its tucked-up feet and Liasis's dangling head and tail were almost brushing the ground. Then the bird soared upwards again and released him with a smug caw.

The prince didn't have time to be frightened. He only fell a foot or two. And, once more, he had a soft landing. This time it was in horse manure. He was right beside a square opening in the stone fortress, big enough for a horse—the stable door. A white mare was grazing in the lush water-grass not very far away. She raised her head to watch the bird fly off, but she didn't seem interested in the snake.

"Lucky," Liasis hissed aloud, but he kept a wary eye on the sky as he slithered off the manure pile and towards the dark doorway.

As far as he could see, there were no guards at this entrance, so he crept cautiously inside and paused to let his eyes adjust to the dimness. Even though the walls, roof, and floor were stone, it looked like a stable, with wooden posts and pegs for harness, a roomy box-stall with fresh bracken on the floor for bedding, and the friendly, warm smell of horse and leather and hay. There was a guard, after all, but she was asleep in a chair. Liasis darted along the wall to the stack of hay in the corner and disappeared into it. When he cautiously stuck his head out, the goblin was still asleep. Her chair was tipped back against the wall, her spear was lying on the floor, and she was snoring, very, very loudly. Right beside her was a big wooden bin, its sloping lid divided into two, each half with a key-hole. The one nearest the guard had a small key in the lock. Liasis recognized them as feed bins. For a moment he couldn't think why anyone would put a lock on a feed bin, but then he realized that Abastor probably couldn't trust the goblins not to eat his horse's oats.

If that was the case, then the bin with the key in the lock wouldn't have oats in it. And Liasis didn't see any other place to lock up a prisoner.

"Poor little Baaawww-biiiiin," a cracked voice echoed from inside it. "Noooobody loooooooves her. Poor little Baaawww-biiiiin. Maybe she'll diiiiiiiie. Maybe she'lll haauuuuunt you, come back and haaauuummmt you. Then you'll be sooooorrrrry. Maybe you'lll cryyyyyy."

"Poor little Baaawww-biiiiin…" She started her song again. Liasis summoned all his courage and darted across the floor, right to the goblin guard's feet.

"Shut up, shut up!" he hissed. "Don't wake the guard."

The guard gave a snorting snore, but didn't open her eyes.

"Prince Snaky?"

"Yes. Be quiet."

"Did you bring my necklace?"

"No! But it's safe. I hid it under the big fallen willow. Be quiet!"

Liasis could see only one way to get to the key. He didn't like it at all, but he'd come this far. He couldn't leave her now. He slithered up the goblin guard's leg, over her greasy, raccoon-skin kilt, up onto her shoulder.

She smacked her lips and scratched her ribs. Liasis held his breath, but the guard settled motionless again. He squirmed onto the edge of the feed bin. Carefully, he gripped the head of the key in his mouth and twisted.

"What are you doing?" Bobbin whispered. "Hurry up."

Liasis couldn't say anything. He just kept twisting, and at last the lock clicked over.

"Hah," he sighed, letting go. "All right, Bobbin. Come on out, carefully."

Rather to his surprise, she did, pushing the lid up slowly, holding it so it didn't bang against the wall, and slinking quietly over the edge. Then, very carefully, she closed and locked it again.

Then, being a goblin, she took a lead-rope off a nearby peg and tied the sleeping guard's ankles together, while Liasis started slithering away. When Bobbin caught up she could hardly stop giggling. She scooped him from the ground and danced a few mad, capering steps across the horse's tiny pasture, until she tripped and they both went sprawling on the grass. The horse curled her lip and then ignored the goblin. Liasis quickly put himself out of reach. He was starting to feel very sorry for the favorite toys of small children.

"You'd make a better goblin lord than Abastor," said Bobbin.

"He'd never bother rescuing anyone, no, not even if they were just doing what he told them and going off scouting, like poor Thimble. You'd never abandon poor Thimble."

"I don't have time to look for Thimble," said Liasis, in a bit of a panic, in case Bobbin decided he should. "What we need to do is get to High Morroway, and ask my father to raise an army to come back here and get rid of Abastor. But first you'll have to sneak in and rescue the toads from the Pit."

"No way," said Bobbin. "I'm not going to get caught and put back in the bin. And your toady knights wouldn't want to be rescued by me anyway, they'd think they were supper." She grinned. "Supper, supper, supper, for poor little Baawww——"

"Shut up, shut up!" hissed Liasis. "No singing! So what do you suggest we do?" he asked, a bit sullenly. He hated to admit it to himself, but Bobbin was probably right.

The goblin squinted around and rubbed at her eyes, which were starting to water in the bright morning light.

"We run away," she said. "Come on, Prince Snaky."

And once more, he was dangling in a goblin fist as Bobbin sprinted along the edge of the island and then suddenly veered off splashing into the swamp. It looked to Liasis as though she had picked the widest, deepest channel of all to wade in, but then he realized the water was barely up to her ankles. She was jogging along a stone causeway hidden just below the water's surface, a road that joined the goblin fortress to the mainland.

As soon as they were out of the swamp and under the cool, dappled green of the forest, Bobbin threw herself beneath a mat of spreading juniper bushes to hide from the sun.

"Look out!" someone hissed.

"Don't move, goblin," whispered a second voice, and Bobbin whimpered as someone pressed the sharp metal spike of a mountain-climbing staff against her chest.

CHAPTER TEN

In which
a prince
gets kissed

The twenty-seven warhorses were exhausted, their ribs showing, their coats dull. Five of them were lame, and they all needed a good rest. There's not much for horses to graze on in a forest; they can't live on twigs. Wren and I spent the evening unharnessing them and picking the burrs and twigs out of their tails. We also gave them a good feed of the grain we found among the knights' supplies. Early in the morning we went on, leaving them to rest and recover along the brook below the dryad's valley, where there was a little grass and where they wouldn't pain her with their iron horseshoes. They all wanted to come with us, of course, no matter how exhausted they were, but I pointed out that even a human and a pony can sneak better than a whole herd of horses, and, since the sorcerer was so powerful, sneaking was probably going to be very important if they ever wanted to see their masters again.

The strange thing was, the horses thought it had only been a couple of days since they came down from the mountains, and that only a night or so had passed while they were trapped in the tangle the sorcerer had made of the forest. It sounded to me as if they had been wandering not only in circles, but in circles of time, too, or in the same little bit of time, over and over. We were going to have to be very sneaky indeed, to steal the prince and the Twenty-Seven Knights back from such a powerful sorcerer.

For two days and part of the morning of the third after we left the dryad's valley we followed the goblin's route through the Forest. On that third morning Thimble began to sniff the air and look around. If he had been a dog, he would have pricked up his ears and wagged his tail. As he wasn't, he just skipped up and down.

"Look, look, look, the charcoal tree!" he said, pointing to an ancient dead elm, a pale naked trunk that had been struck by lightning and left with a wide streak of charcoal from the top to the ground.

"So you know where you are now?" Wren asked. "Good. It's time you told us how we can get into the den, and where we'll be likely to find the prince."

"Don't know," said Thimble, turning sulky. "Don't want to find the stupid prince."

"Well, we do," I said.

"Lord Abastor'll be mad."

"I'll be mad if you don't tell us," Wren said. "And then I'll never, ever make you bannock again. Come on."

She led the way along what was turning into quite a well-used track, which wound through the ancient trees, dividing and meeting up with other paths. They were all littered with broken branches, shattered bits of crockery jars, rotten fish heads, bones, and that sort of thing, so it was easy to tell goblins used them regularly. Thimble pattered along behind us, grumbling and sniffling. After a while he fell silent, which was a relief. Wren kept following the widest, most well-used-looking of the paths, but at one fork she hesitated and looked back.

"Which way, Thimble?" she asked. "Thimble?"

I looked around too. I should have known. The goblin was gone.

"Little pest," Wren said, but we both knew it was far worse than that.

"You should've let that black mare trample him," said Ash.

"We've got to move faster, or we'll find a welcoming party when we get there." Wren hauled herself up onto Ash's back amid the baskets, and gave me a hand up, too. "No matter how bad Thimble's sense of direction is, he probably knows all the shortcuts around here. Pick a path."

Ash snorted and broke into a canter down the right-hand track.

"I was talking to Torrie, actually," said Wren.

But I thought Ash had made the right choice. This path did look wider, tramped by many feet until it was almost a narrow road. It sloped steadily downhill until we rounded a corner and saw what looked like a brilliant green meadow stretching out before us, splashed with vivid spikes of purple loosestrife in flower. Ash tossed his head and stretched into a gallop.

"Whoa! Whoa!" I shouted.

"Why whoa?" he asked. "Look at all that grass. It's going to be so nice to run on, and roll in, and eat—"

"It's a swamp!" I said. "I know where we are now! That's the Great Musquash."

"Great what?" Wren asked, as Ash slowed to a jolting trot.

"The Great Musquash," I said. "It's a swamp in the Wild Forest. Some dwarves started to make a small palace out of a rock island in the middle of it, but that was a long time ago. It's been ages since I've been here. It hasn't changed much," I added, "except there didn't use to be goblins."

"Well, there's your rock island." Wren pointed. "How much do you want to bet it's a goblin fortress now?"

"Not even a piece of cheese," I said.

"Water grass is good too," said Ash hopefully. "It's probably time for lunch."

"No eating yet," I told him. And to Wren I said, "Let's get out of sight."

We found a little grove of hackmatack trees where Ash could wait, well hidden, although he grumbled about the thin, wiry grass that grew beneath them. Then Wren and I cautiously followed the path to the water's edge, where we crawled under some prickly, sharp-scented junipers to spy out the land.

"There!" hissed Wren, pointing, and I followed her finger. Thimble was already on the island, easy to recognize by his hat of dry fern leaves. We could see him climbing along a narrow path, disappearing out of sight around the eastern end.

"Look!" I said. There was a big, square doorway facing us at the western end of the island, and a goblin dashed out of it, leaping around a white mountain horse that was grazing there. The goblin fell down, got up, and came running towards us, splashing through shallow water. As she came closer, I could see she was carrying a snake.

"Probably stealing someone else's dinner," I said. "Just keep quiet and she'll go on by."

But she didn't.

"Look out!" I hissed a warning as the goblin, reaching dry land, spun on her heel and flung herself in on top of us.

Wren rolled over and forced the goblin against the ground, holding her staff tucked under her arm like a lance, with the spike resting on the goblin's gray chest. "Don't move, goblin!"

The goblin dropped her lunch, a garter snake, and it slithered away. Then the snake reared its head up and looked at me.

Wren was staring at it too, squinting, as if the light were overly bright. "Torrie. . ." she said.

Funny colored eyes for a snake, I thought. They were blue. And it smelled sort of like, well, as though someone had been sick on it. It smelled like really nasty, ill-wishing sorcery—sorcery that was meant to make people suffer.

"Let her go," hissed the snake. "Let her go right now, or I'll bite you."

"That snake's sort of, tangled up in something," Wren said slowly. "Kind of. . .strands of mucky light. And it stinks."

"I've been in the swamp," said the snake indignantly. "And then that crow dropped me in the manure pile. It's not my fault."

I reached out my hand and gently picked up the snake. It coiled around my wrist and flicked its tongue nervously.

"You can't eat that snake!" the goblin howled at me.

"I think there's a spell on it," said Wren, and she put out her hand to the snake. "Um...snake?"

The snake slithered from my hand to hers. "*You might not recognize him when you find him.*" Wren quoted what Rookfeather the minstrel had told us, so many weeks ago. "Your name's not Liasis, is it, snake? Um, Your Highness?"

"You can tell?" The snake wriggled around her arm, its tongue an excited black blur. "You can tell! Look, we've got to get away from here, there's a sorcerer and—"

"What's he saying, Torrie?" Wren asked.

"Oh," said the snake, sounding disappointed. "She can't understand me. What's she doing here, anyway?"

"I can," I said. Odd that he seemed to recognize Wren, but I had more important things to ask. "Are you Prince Liasis?"

Of course, he was.

THE PRINCE'S FIRST IDEA was that we should head for High Morroway as fast as we could go and find some sorcerers and an army to defeat Abastor and rescue the toads. That was before we told Liasis and Bobbin about Thimble. We all knew the goblin was bound to have gone straight to Abastor. The sorcerer was probably already looking for Wren and me.

"That stupid, stupid, stupid baby brother!" Bobbin shrieked. "I'm goin' to box his ears and pull his toes and spank him, that stupid! Now we're goin' to get caught again!"

"There's certainly no chance of making it back to High Morroway," Wren said. "And sitting under a bush right beside the goblins' main highway isn't a good idea either." She looked at me and raised her eyebrows. "So, is this where the adventure gets really interesting, Torrie?"

"Very likely," I answered.

"You really should have run away to play the fiddle," Wren told the snake, which was still coiled around her arm. "It would have made everything so much easier."

"What?" Liasis asked. He looked at me.

"Never mind," I told him.

"I know a place," Bobbin said, and she tugged at Wren's sleeve. "A good place, a secret place. We can hide there."

"Are you any more trustworthy than your baby brother?" Wren asked sternly.

"We can trust her," the prince said. "Tell her, Torrie. Bobbin rescued me, and when Abastor would have caught me, she threw me to safety."

"Yeah," said Bobbin. "You listen to Prince Snaky. We're friends, him and me. Pals."

"The prince says he trusts her," I told Wren.

Wren and I looked at one another. We looked at the goblin. Goblins always look rather sly and shifty, but this particular goblin was looking particularly sly. Wren nodded at me.

"All right," she said. "We'll head for your secret place, Bobbin."

But she and I were going to keep a sharp lookout for treachery.

We set off, following the goblin, and collected Ash from the hackmatack grove on the way.

The pony was not impressed with our new companion.

"Oh, good," he said. "Another goblin. Tell Wren if she wants to keep pets, Torrie, I've always thought kittens would be nice."

It didn't take long to get to Bobbin's secret place, which was a broken ring of stones on a nearby hilltop.

"Ah," I said. "I remember when this was a tower, long ago."

It was all ruins now. You'd hardly have been able to tell it had ever been a tower; it was just a jumble of squared gray stones, overgrown with moss and the roots of sugar maples.

"This isn't secret, though," Wren pointed out.

"Stupids," said Bobbin. "You can't run away from Lord Abastor on a pony. You can't hide in a ruin. He'll find you with sorcery. He'll catch you and turn you into toads, too, and throw you in the Pit with the others, and I'll get locked up again. You're going to have to fight him, and this is a good place for that."

"Fight him!" Wren and I both exclaimed. Liasis hissed.

"We can't fight a sorcerer," said Wren. "Look what he did to the Twenty-Seven Royal Knights! I'm not a knight. I don't even have a sword."

"Goin' to have to fight him," said Bobbin smugly. "Sooner or later. Better be sooner, before you get scared."

"Hm," I said, looking around the ruins of the tower. There was only one gap in the tumbled ridge of stone, where the tower door had been. A big maple tree grew to one side of it. There was no dryad living in it, which was a pity, because a big strong maple dryad would have been a help. But you probably don't need me to tell you dryads don't like to live around goblin dens.

Wren was letting Liasis flow from one hand to the other, looking thoughtful herself.

"If we could change Liasis back, at least there'd be four of us," she said. "Plus Ash, is five. How many goblins live on the island, Bobbin?"

Bobbin scratched her head. "Maybe a hundred."

Wren groaned. Then she grinned. "Well, that's only about twenty each. Does magic really work like in fairy tales, Torrie?"

"Sometimes," I said.

Wren wrinkled up her nose. "Sorry, Your Highness," she said. "It's worth a try. It'd be twenty-five goblins each, without you." And she scrunched her eyes shut, closed her fist around Liasis, and kissed him right on his blunt nose.

"Erk!" said Liasis, squirming frantically.

Wren opened one eye cautiously, and then the other.

"No good," she sighed, setting the prince down on the ground. "Just as well. You'd probably have to marry me and give me half your kingdom."

"Let me try!" said Bobbin, and she snatched up the snake.

"No!" Liasis shrieked, as much as a snake can shriek.

"No kissing! Torrie! Tell them to stop!"

Bobbin planted a smacking, slobbery kiss on the top of his head.

"Stop kissing the prince," I said. "You're making too much noise and I'm trying to think."

Liasis escaped and shot into a crack between the stones.

Wren pulled herself to her feet and started twirling her staff, thrusting and whacking at imagined enemies, blocking imaginary strikes back at her, doing the quarterstaff exercises she usually did in the mornings. For her, it was a way of thinking, sort of like meditating, but sweatier. The prince stuck his head from between the rocks to watch, but he kept half an eye on Bobbin.

"Hah!" said Wren. "I wonder… Liasis, Your Highness, come out here a moment."

Liasis disappeared again. "No."

Wren sat down on the ground again. "No more kissing," she said. "It was a silly idea, anyway. Nothing's ever that easy. But I can see this spell on you, and I want to take another look at it."

"She can really see it?" Liasis asked me. "I thought she was a pedlar, not a sorcerer. I mean, she tried to sell me a packet of buttons, last time we met."

"When *did* you meet?" I asked. "Wren said she'd never met you."

"I didn't tell her my name." His voice had a smile in it, remembering. "I didn't need any buttons, but I bought an ornament she'd made, a tin fish."

"You don't need any buttons now, either," I pointed out. "Wren's not exactly a trained sorcerer—yet. But already she's good at detecting spells and understanding what they're doing. Let her take a look."

The prince crawled over to Wren and let her pick him up again. She ran a finger over his scales, talking to herself.

"It's all knotted around him. I can't pull it off. It must be… holding on, somehow. So if we could make it stick on to something else…"

"Pull what off? Make what stick on?" Liasis coiled and twisted, looking at his own back, which is pretty easy for a snake to do.

"The spell," said Wren, in a distracted kind of way, setting the prince down on the moss beside her.

I watched Wren, wondering.

"Maybe . . ." Wren felt around in her pockets and pulled out some fine copper wire, a yellow ribbon, and her pliers. Her hands started to work.

I almost held my breath. The fancy that took shape over the next hour was mostly made of short lengths of wire held together with loops and loose twists. It looked only vaguely human, and then only when you looked at it the right way. The yellow ribbon wound through it, making no particular pattern. Wren felt in the pocket of her shirt, inside her tunic, and took out the folded scrap of red silk. Working very carefully, she tied the blond hair into the snaggle of wires. Then she took a deep breath.

Bobbin, who had curled up in a shady corner, woke up with a snort. "What 'cha doing, making rabbit snares?"

"Sh!" I said, but Wren didn't even hear.

"Now," Wren said, like a sigh. Holding the bit of bespelled cobweb and the snake scales delicately between the first two fingers of her right hand, she ran those fingers over Liasis's long, snaky back. Then she drew her hand away from him, running it over the funny little wire figure she had made, twisting the cobweb and the scales into the fancy. I could see flares and flickers of muddy light following the path her fingers made. It was as though she was pulling that light off Liasis, slowly and delicately, and wrapping it around the fancy. And then all the sparks of muddy light were flickering over the fancy, and none were on the prince any more.

Liasis twitched, and gasped, and fell over. Bobbin squealed. Wren jumped to her feet, and so did Liasis—a tall, blue-eyed boy, a year or so younger than Wren, with straw-colored hair and a crooked nose from a riding accident. He was a bit unsteady because he was so unused to his feet.

"I *felt* that," said Liasis. "I could feel that...that snakiness... peeling off me. What did you do?"

"I'm not sure," Wren admitted, looking at the fancy in her hand. "It just felt—like it was working."

The fancy didn't look like a wobbly-jointed human figure any more. The wires had somehow changed their positions. It was a long, flexible snake, and the yellow ribbon wound along it like a garter snake's stripe. And I was going to make sure Wren threw it into the first swift-flowing stream we crossed, to let the water pound and pummel the foul magic away to nothing.

Then Wren looked up again. "Oh!" she said. "I do know you, after all. You never said you were a prince. You bought one of my fancies." Then she said, *"Oh!"* once more, and started to get up and turn around so quickly she stumbled on her bad foot and fell, her face blushing bright red—not because she'd fallen, but because the prince didn't have on a stitch of clothing.

"Sorry," said Wren. "Um, I have a change of clothes in one of those baskets. Um, Your Highness. They'll probably fit you."

"Thank you," said Liasis, in that sort of stiff, awkward voice people use when they're really embarrassed.

Bobbin giggled.

"You can turn your back, too," said Liasis. "You're a *girl!*"

"Seen you naked lots of times before," sniggered Bobbin, but she plunked herself down on the ground by Wren. The two of them looked at one another and they both giggled.

Liasis gave a snort of laughter, getting over his embarrassment. After all, it was one of those accidents that could happen to anyone who changes shape in a public place. Just ask the next werewolf you meet.

"Before doesn't count," said the prince. "I had scales on, then."

"Torrie?" called Ash, from where he was browsing the grass in the old doorway. "Trouble."

I climbed up on the stones to look down through the forest.

"Hurry up," I called back to Liasis. "Here come Abastor and about thirty goblins. Wren, if you could thump the sorcerer with your staff first thing, we might have a chance."

Probably Liasis had never gotten dressed so quickly in his life, not even on the coldest February morning. Wren was looking around the ruined foundation of the tower, her eyes bright, on fire with the power you get from doing some great thing successfully.

"All right," Wren said, and she took a deep breath. "We don't have much time. Now, this is what we're going to do…"

"No killin' goblins," said Bobbin firmly. "You can do thwacking, and thumping, and kicking, and biting, but no killing. They're *my* goblins."

Nobody made any promises. I hoped it wouldn't come to that, but if it was us or the goblins…

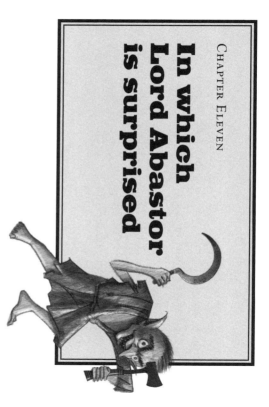

CHAPTER ELEVEN

In which Lord Abastor is surprised

I suppose kings and generals, after they've arranged their troops and are waiting for the enemy, must get that same nervous, squirmy feeling in the stomach as I had that day among the stones of the old tower. It wasn't even my plan. It was Wren's, but I couldn't think of a better one in the few moments we had, and I felt just as responsible as if it had been mine. I had gotten her into this. Well, actually it had been that arrogant minstrel, Rookfeather. I still didn't know what sort of game she was playing, and why she had wanted Wren and me to go after the prince. I expected her to show up as soon as we found Liasis, but perhaps that rook I had seen in the foothills hadn't been anything to do with her. After all, we saw lots of wrens in the forest, and not a single one of them was spying for Wren.

Wren was nervously twirling her quarterstaff again. I could imagine the thoughts going through her mind. Had she really put all her forces in the best possible place? Was the enemy going to show up where she expected him to? Would the enemy's troops behave the way she wanted them to, or were they going to think for themselves and take her by surprise instead?

It was just as well neither of us had had any lunch.

"This had better work, Torrie," Liasis whispered nervously.

"Do you have any idea what worms taste like?"

"They're not my favorite food," I admitted. "Maybe you should have tried beetles. Very sweet and crunchy, if you get the right kind. Junebugs are the best, but——"

"Shh!" warned Wren.

"This is a bad idea," said Bobbin suddenly. "Maybe we should just run away."

"Fighting Abastor was *your* idea," Liasis pointed out. "Now be quiet."

"He's goin' to turn me into a swallow! I don't wanna be a bird, I'm afraid of heights!"

"Better than a snake," said Liasis. There was a muffled squeak from Bobbin as the prince put his hand over her mouth. The two of them were crouching among the jumbled rocks opposite the grassy gap in the stones where the doorway had once been.

"Here he comes," I warned softly.

Lord Abastor led the way up towards the ruins, striding through the maple trees ahead of his goblins. It was the first time I'd seen him, and though I was peering out from behind fallen stones, with lots of ginseng and may-apple plants in the way, I could see enough. The sorcerer looked so much like Rookfeather the minstrel that I almost gasped aloud in surprise. In fact, for a moment I thought he *was* Rookfeather, wearing a false beard, and Wren confessed later that she had thought so, too. But where Rookfeather's usual expression had seemed both thoughtful and amused, this man looked as if he spent most of his time being proud and angry.

"Pedlar!" he shouted. "Old Thing! I know you're here somewhere."

Thimble slunk nervously behind him. There was more squeaking and rustling beyond the stones. I found out afterwards that Bobbin tried to jump up to yell at her brother, and Liasis sat on her to keep her still.

The goblins were scattered in a loose pack behind Abastor. They made a lot of noise, trampling things and snapping branches back at one another and squealing when one of the snapped branches hit.

Not yet, I thought, as he drew nearer. Not yet.

When the sorcerer was only a few steps from the ruined tower, Liasis jumped up onto what was left of the ruined wall. He raised his chin and folded his arms and stood there, proud and scruffy in Wren's patched trousers and shirt.

"Are you looking for me?" he asked.

Bobbin's head popped up over the stones. "Nyah!" She crossed her eyes and stuck out her tongue before she disappeared again.

"You!" Abastor bellowed at the prince. "What the…how…?" And without noticing anything else at all, he took two long strides into the gap in the stones, his fingers already flickering in complicated patterns and his lips muttering, preparing a spell.

The prince swallowed and sweat beaded his forehead, but he stood his ground. And, as Abastor took one more step under the giant maple, Wren's arm swung down from the branch she was lying on, her staff tucked along her forearm, and thumped the sorcerer on the chin—not with the pointy end, but the other.

Abastor's head jerked up, his eyes rolled back, and he slumped senseless to the ground.

Wren dropped down from the tree, landing on her good left foot and her staff. "Quick, quick," she said. "Torrie, rope!"

"And a gag," I said, rolling Lord Abastor onto his side and making sure he was still breathing. For a moment I'd been a bit worried. It's very easy to kill someone, even without meaning to, by hitting them on the head. Wren had insisted that she knew just how hard to hit someone's chin to knock them out. She'd had a bit of practice on goblins, after all, during her travels alone into the mountains. Abastor's teeth had clacked together with a noise we'd all heard and I think he might have bitten his tongue, but he was alive.

We shoved one of Wren's spare socks into his mouth (it wasn't a clean one) and tied it there, and then we tied his hands behind his back. He wouldn't be chanting or casting any spells.

"Showed you! Showed you!" yelped Bobbin, dancing around him. "Lock me in the feed bin! Now you're sorry! And Thimble, you stupid, stupid numbskull——!"

She grabbed her brother by his ears, shook him, and then hugged him.

"Get out of the way!" shouted Wren, and Liasis grabbed both goblins and pulled them back into the ring of stones.

Wren took a deep breath, standing in front of Abastor's body, her staff resting lightly in her hands. I sprang up on the stones beside her. "Stay," I heard Liasis ordering the two goblins, as if he were talking to a pair of puppies, and then he climbed up on the stones on the other side, leaving Wren lots of room. He held a short length of fallen branch like a club.

The thirty or so goblins who had been following the sorcerer hesitated.

"Stupids!" shrieked Bobbin, scrambling up beside Liasis and shaking her fist. "You really want this stupid sorcerer for a goblin lord? He can't even beat a skinny little human in a fight!"

"Hey," muttered Wren. "I'm not skinny."

"Even I'm smarter 'n him! He's only half Fair Folk, you know, hardly an Old Thing at all, and anyway, what kind of a goblin lord is a stupid snooty fairy, or a stupid greedy human?"

Half Fair Folk? That explained why Abastor had been able to understand Liasis when he was a snake. That explained a lot. The Fair Folk are very proud, powerful beings, strong in the kinds of magic we Old Things possess. They look a lot like very beautiful humans, tall and graceful, so it isn't too surprising that every now and then a fairy (which is a human name for the Fair Folk), and a human will marry and have a family. Their children usually have a strong talent for human sorcery, as well as a bit of Old Thing magic, and sometimes they live almost as long as us Old Things, too.

And often they don't look quite human. Humans being humans—afraid of anyone different—the half-fairy humans have trouble being accepted in human society. And, Fair Folk being very proud Fair Folk, half-human children are never quite made to feel at home among them, either.

It can be rather a lonely life.

"Goblins should be ruled by goblins!" Bobbin shrieked. "Goblins for goblins!"

"Yeah," called Thimble weakly. "Um, right." But he stayed hidden behind the stones.

"That human girl killed Lord Abastor!" yelled the biggest of the goblins. "She stole our prisoner. She's corrumpted Bobbin!"

"Corrumpted?" Wren asked. "I don't think there's any such word. Do you mean corrupted?"

"Yeah, Fleabane, you stupid goblin!" Bobbin chimed in.

"Get the humans!" howled the big goblin, and he rushed forward, waving a stone axe. Another big one was right behind him with a broken human sword in her hand.

I think they'd both seen a sudden chance to become the next goblin lord. Goblins usually do follow the strongest, loudest goblin. It saves thinking. (Some humans, sad to say, do the same thing.)

A wind started to mutter in the leaves of the trees. As I think I've told you, the Wild Forest is *mine*, in a way no other place on earth is. I belong to it. It listens to me. And deep, deep down, I was growing angry.

The songbirds fell silent. Liasis raised his club. Bobbin shrieked and dove for cover.

Wren stood square and steady with her staff held in both hands and, as Fleabane, the goblin with the axe, raced at her, she swept the longer end in a swift arc. The staff struck the goblin crossways in the belly, knocking him flying. He landed with a thump and a whooshing groan. Liasis bashed the one with the broken sword in the arm so that she screeched and dropped her weapon. She tried to turn and run away so quickly that her feet got tangled up. She fell, rolled down the hill, and stayed there, curled up into a little ball against the trunk of a tree. The goblins who had started scrambling up the hill behind them halted again, looking embarrassed and confused. After all, Wren had just defeated two would-be goblin lords in a row, and Liasis might have broken the arm of another one. That sort of thing makes even a goblin stop and think.

The wind growled angrily, blowing dirt and dust into their faces, and the forest felt suddenly dark and dangerous. The goblins huddled close together. Clammy tendrils of fog stretched out of the earth, coiling around them.

"Surrender!" shouted Bobbin, popping up again. "Surrender to the Great Goblin Lord Liasis and What's Her Name the mighty Goblin-Whacker!"

Wren and Liasis looked at one another.

"I think I liked it better when she just called me Prince Snaky," said Liasis, and he tapped Bobbin on the head. "Weren't you just saying you didn't want a human goblin lord?" he asked.

"Okay, surrender to Bobbin, the great human-tamer!" Bobbin shouted, dancing around.

"Yeah, Bobbin for goblin lord!" squealed Thimble.

The goblins shuffled and shoved and finally one, wearing a ragged pair of human trousers with the legs rolled up, was pushed out to the front.

"We've got you outnumbered," he said, a bit nervously. "Why should we be the ones that surrender?"

"Cause you're surrounded," said Bobbin. "Cause What's Her Name, Pedlar Girl here, is a mighty sorcerer. Who do you think broke Abastor's enchantment on Prince Snaky? Who do you think is goin' to change you all into earthworms and feed ya to the toady knights?"

"We're not surrounded," objected another goblin, as the one in trousers tried to fight his way back into the center of the crowd.

"Ask Wren if I can charge them now, Torrie," Ash whinnied.

The goblins looked behind them, to where Ash had quietly sneaked around the hill. One mountain pony wouldn't stand much chance against nearly thirty goblins, if they stuck together, but with his ears flattened down to his skull and his yellow teeth bared, and with the way he was pawing slowly at the ground, now with one front hoof, now with the other, he looked as dangerous as a whole cavalry charge.

"Throw down your weapons," said Wren sternly. "Give us the twenty-seven toads who were the Royal Knights of High Morroway, and promise never to raid in High Morroway again. And then we'll go and you can choose your own goblin lord."

"I'd suggest you choose Bobbin," Liasis added. "She's the only one of you who was smart enough to realize that following Lord Abastor was a bad idea."

"But I want to charge them, Torrie," said Ash. "Why can't I? Just a little?"

"Not when they're surrendering," I said. "It's not honorable."

"Neither are goblins," the pony grumbled.

"Throw your weapons down, now," Wren repeated. "Or I won't be able to stop my savage steed. He's got a taste for goblin blood. Just ask Thimble here."

Thimble squeaked and nodded.

"Do as Wren says," I said quietly. Just that. But the goblins looked around at the dark and shivering forest, and they started laying down their weapons.

"Dummies!" said Bobbin happily. "Lookit Abastor—he can't stop us now. Think of all that loot he's got locked up—cheese and sausages and plum puddings and ham pies and coriander beer. Let's feast!"

She bounded down among the goblins, whacking this one and that on the back in what was mostly a friendly fashion. Thimble capered after her.

The goblins gave a ragged cheer.

"Bobbin for chief!"

"Bobbin for goblin lord!"

"Hooray for Lord Bobbin!"

"*Lady* Bobbin!" she corrected.

Even the two who had been hurt were helped up. They stumbled off into the crowd, joining in the cheering.

"Bobbin!" Liasis shouted.

She waved at him from the middle of the band. "See ya, Snaky Prince!"

"No, wait! We need the Twenty-Seven Knights."

"Sure! Toads is no good to eat, anyway!"

"And don't forget, your…you-know-what…is under the big fallen willow."

Bobbin waved again.

Ash could stand it no more. When the gang of goblins went trotting and yelping past right in front of him, he reared up on his hind legs, whinnying and beating the air with his fore-legs, and then he dropped to the ground and charged.

It was only a little charge, and he didn't actually trample or bite any of them, but the goblins broke into a panicked run, squealing and wailing. Except Bobbin. She jumped up on a stump, whooping and laughing and cheering Ash on. Then she ran off after them.

Ash trotted up the hill to rejoin the rest of us, looking very pleased with himself.

"Did you see me charge, Torrie? Ask Wren if she saw my charge. That was pretty good, eh? Just like a warhorse."

I patted his shoulder. "Very nice."

"Can I borrow Ash and his baskets?" Liasis asked. "I think I'd better follow the goblins and collect the toads myself. Bobbin means well, but I don't want there to be some sort of nasty accident."

"Good idea," said Wren, putting Ash's lead rein in the prince's hand.

"Bad idea," said Ash. "I don't want to carry baskets of slimy toads all the way back to High Morroway."

"That's right," I said. "Toads need to stay damp. You'd better put some wet moss in the baskets, Liasis."

Ash groaned and gave me a reproachful look.

"Nobody makes warhorses carry soggy baskets of toads around," he was grumbling, as Liasis led him off.

AND THEN IT WAS JUST WREN and Lord Abastor and I, alone. Birds sang again, and the trailing fingers of cold fog that had begun to coil around the goblins burned away. The leaves fluttered in what was only a mild summer breeze and the afternoon sun slanted down like liquid honey, raising warm, brown scents from the rich black earth.

"Oh, Torrie," sighed Wren. She knelt down on the ground beside Lord Abastor. "I've never been so scared in my life. I thought I was going to end up a toad for sure. And what happened to the forest, just then? It looked like...like all the fairy tales, the frightening ones people tell on the long winter nights, where the Wild Forest is so dark and dangerous and people get trapped and lost and…"

"Oh well," I said vaguely. "It's not all summer afternoons, you know."

We Old Things, the most powerful of us, anyhow, are part of our land, and it's part of us. And of the Old Things of the Wild Forest, I'm *the* Old Thing: the first, the oldest. But that's not something I wanted to discuss, even with Wren.

"People, even goblins, tend to bring their own adventures with them, really," I added. "Sometimes they wake up very dangerous things, in the Forest's heart. Don't worry about it. What are you going to do with your prisoner?"

"He's awake," said Wren.

He was. Lord Abastor was awake, and glowering at us.

"What should I do with him?" she asked.

"It's up to you," I said. "You captured him."

"I suppose we should take him back to High Morroway so they can put him on trial for kidnapping the prince," she said. "It's going to be difficult. We can't starve him, but if we take the gag out of his mouth, he's going to try to cast a spell. Couldn't you, well," and Wren looked around at the forest, almost a little nervously. "Couldn't *you* do something?"

I shook my head. I wasn't saying I could, and I wasn't saying I couldn't.

"I won't," I said. "Lord Abastor is not the Wild Forest's problem. He needs to be taken away." I thought for a moment. "Maybe you could put a spell on him, to stop him doing magic," I suggested.

Lord Abastor's green eyes blazed.

"He doesn't like that idea," Wren said, with a bit of a grin. "Maybe it's a good one." Then she looked serious again. "How?" she asked. "Torrie, how did I change Liasis back? It was just a weird idea I had, because I could see that mucky light on him, but how could I do it? That was...that was sorcery, wasn't it? Real sorcery."

"It was," I said, and I patted her knee.

"Oh," she said. There was long moment of silence. "So what do I do? Go on selling ribbons and buttons and fancies?"

"If you like," I said. "You can do whatever you want. And your fancies really are charms, you know, just the way people believe. They do carry good feelings. They do good. I think that's what saved Ash, when he fell down the cliff."

"Really? But if I can do that without knowing it...I could... I could do something really bad without knowing it, too."

"You might," I admitted. "I don't think it's very likely. You don't seem to have a lot of bad feelings in you. But even so, you might."

"I'm dangerous!"

"Well, everyone's dangerous, in one way or another."

"What do you think I should do, Torrie?" she asked.

Giving people advice is always dangerous. Sometimes they take it. I thought carefully.

"You didn't want to be a cobbler's apprentice, but you could probably learn a lot as a sorcerer's apprentice. It would have to be the right sort of sorcerer, though. Liasis could ask his stepmother to introduce you to her uncle, the sultan's Court Enchanter in Callipepla. But you're not the type to settle down at court, either. Wearing velvet robes and riding pedigreed horses." I was remembering what Ash had said about what he thought all sorcerers were like.

Wren made a face.

"There are all sorts of sorcerers around," I said. "If you wander long enough, you'll find the right teacher for you."

Lord Abastor grunted and kicked his heels on the ground. I think he might have been a bit annoyed to hear that Liasis had been disenchanted by someone who wasn't even an apprentice sorcerer. Or maybe he wanted to offer to teach Wren himself. I wasn't about to take the sock out of his mouth to find out.

Leaves fluttered and rustled, and we both looked up as a black bird dropped out of the sky. A rook. *Ah*, I thought. Now maybe we'd find out what the minstrel was up to.

The bird landed on the stones and peered at Lord Abastor, tilting its head from side to side. Abastor grunted and squeaked and tried to roll away. Wren put her foot out and stopped him.

"He deserved it," I said, in case the rook was going to say this was no way to treat a person.

"He always does," said the rook, a bit sadly, and something about the way she spoke made me realize it wasn't actually a rook's mind inside that body.

"Oh," I groaned. "Not another one. I thought you were just Rookfeather's pet, a tame spy. Who are you? Did he enchant you, too, or was it the minstrel?"

The rook walked away along the stones, and then, with a swirl of black feathers and red and green silk, she hopped down. The minstrel Rookfeather stood before us, tucking two long, shiny feathers back into her hair.

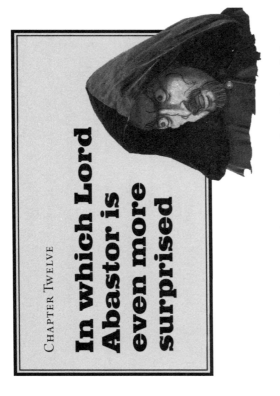

CHAPTER TWELVE

In which Lord Abastor is even more surprised

Rookfeather gave the sorcerer another look, and then turned away, leaning against a tree with her back to us, as if she really didn't want to see Abastor tied up there on the ground.

"Er . . ." said Wren, and she looked at me.

"You seem to have a difficulty," the minstrel said.

"Er," said Wren again. "Well, yes. Um, did you just—"

"It's a simple one to solve," said Rookfeather. "If—*If* some-one wanted to stop Abastor causing any more problems for a while, and *if* some very strong young sorcerer had taught her-self an entirely new way of working transformation spells, well, I don't think even a powerful sorcerer like him could do much magic in a small, weak shape. Some small bird, for example."

"But I don't really know—"Wren began, at the same time as I said, "Why don't *you*—"

"*I think*," said Rookfeather, interrupting us both. "That it might be a good idea to do it quickly, if anyone was going to. Before he figures out a way to cast a spell, even tied up and gagged."

Lord Abastor was definitely looking quite angry and popeyed, and not at all like a man who thought the fight was over.

"But——" said Wren.

"A small bird," said Rookfeather, "would be just the thing." And she sat down on the ground, still with her back to us, took her harp out of its sack, and began tuning it. Faint, plinking notes floated around us, and then settled into a slow, sad melody.

"Hmph," said Wren. "Torrie?"

I shrugged. "I suppose it's worth a try," I said. "We have to do something with him."

"Erffff," grunted Lord Abastor, managing to make a noise at last.

"Sooner rather than later," I added.

"I don't want to do that kind of sorcery, though," said Wren. "It's wrong. That spell on Liasis, it looked wrong, it smelled wrong. Rotten and ugly."

"It's not so much what you do, as why you're doing it," I told her. "If you're not doing it full of hatred and anger and wanting to hurt someone, it'll be a different kind of magic from Abastor's."

Wren took a deep breath and nodded. "All right then."

She felt around in her pockets and pulled out some odds and ends of wire and ribbon, using her pliers to bend and twist the wires. Then she took out her knife and snicked off a lock of Lord Abastor's hair.

"Erff ufff urrr!" he said.

"Just be glad we're not taking you back to High Morroway," I said. "Think what King Boiga would want to do to you."

Wren pulled several feathers from the band of her hat, looking them over carefully before putting all but one of them back.

"What is it?" I asked her, trying to guess. But, like most of her fancies, it was very hard to see a particular shape in it unless you looked at it the right way.

"Wait and see if it works."

Wren was starting to look a bit pale and tired, with shadows under her eyes. Working sorcery can be very exhausting, and not only was Wren new to it, but the thing she had done, and was trying to do again—actually transforming a living being into something else—was terribly difficult. I didn't tell her that. Sometimes hard things are easier to do if nobody tells you beforehand all the reasons that you shouldn't be able to do them.

I noticed that Rookfeather hadn't told her how hard it was, either. Maybe, I thought, the minstrel wanted to test Wren, and find out how talented she really was by setting her a challenge. Even if she failed, how she tried to make the spell would probably tell another sorcerer a lot about how she did magic… another sorcerer who might be thinking Wren would make a good apprentice?

Ah, I thought. Perhaps that was what Rookfeather was up to. Perhaps that had been her plan all along.

As it turned out, I was almost entirely wrong.

It didn't take Wren nearly as long to make this fancy as it had to make the one she had used to change Liasis back. It was only about a quarter of an hour later when she held up a little, glimmering thing, swinging on a loop of strong thread. Abastor's hair was part of it, and so was the single brown feather. It flickered with light and movement, quick and brown—not a grubby, ugly color but a rich nut brown, with flashes of white. Almost…yes, I could almost see the bird in it, a quick, chirpy, brown and white sparrow.

Wren cut off a second lock of Abastor's hair. His face was red with rage. I gave her an encouraging smile.

"Here goes," she said, which most sorcerers would probably tell her was not the sort of thing to say when starting to work a spell. It just doesn't sound very mysterious or magical.

She held the sparrow-fancy swinging from one hand and, with the other, she used the little twist of hair she had just cut like a paintbrush. She stroked it over the fancy, frowning with concentration, putting all the force of her will into it. Then she brushed the hair over Lord Abastor. The flickers of brown and white light flowed along the line she traced, following the brush of hair. They flashed and sparked and whirled like a snowstorm of downy feathers, and then, with a shrill cry, Lord Abastor flung himself at Wren's face, stabbing with a tiny beak, clawing with tiny talons. He was a sparrow.

I reached out and caught him, holding him gently but firmly between my hands so that he couldn't hurt himself by struggling.

"Easy, easy," I said, as he tried to beat his wings. "It's probably better than being a snake or a toad. At least you can fly. And I'm not even going to say it serves you right. But it does."

"Let me go!" he twittered. "She hit me! My jaw hurts. My beak hurts! And she's got no right to go enchanting people."

"Neither do you," I pointed out.

"Is he all right?" Wren asked anxiously.

"He's angry. His beak is sore."

"Well, I'm sorry," said Wren, talking to the sparrow. "But maybe this'll make you stop and think before you go putting spells on any more people, or kidnapping them."

"We can always hope," said Rookfeather. I hadn't noticed when she had stopped playing her harp, but there she was, looking down at us.

"This is all your fault!" the sparrow said.

Rookfeather raised an eyebrow. "I didn't do anything. I can't. You know I can't."

"You told her to do this. You're not supposed to do things like that."

The minstrel shrugged. "I was just thinking out loud. I didn't tell her to do anything." Then she grinned. She really did have pointy eyeteeth, like fox. "It seems to me they could have dragged you back to King Boiga like a parcel, if they'd wanted to. And what would little Demansia have thought of you then?"

"It's none of your business. Let me go!" Abastor pecked at my hand.

"Leave Wren alone, or I'll make roast sparrow for supper," I warned him. I opened my hands and he fluttered away to perch on a twig over our heads.

I got to my feet and gave Wren a hand up. We both kept a cautious eye on Abastor in case he flew at her face again, but he only flicked his tail and ruffled his feathers. When Rookfeather reached out a finger and gently smoothed some crooked feathers, he shuffled his feet and looked sulky.

"He's your brother?" Wren guessed. "He looks like you."

"Or he used to," I murmured.

Rookfeather nodded. "He's a bit of a problem, sometimes."

"Yes," said Wren. "I can see he would be."

"What did you mean when you said that you *couldn't* do anything?" I asked. "And he said you weren't supposed to do things like that."

Rookfeather looked at her brother again and shrugged.

"She's not allowed to!" Abastor chirped. "She's forbidden to do anything against me!"

"He's my younger brother," Rookfeather said softly. "Like your goblin friend with her brother. I'm supposed to look after him."

"That's ridiculous," said Wren. "He's grown up."

I looked at the minstrel thoughtfully. "How long have you been looking after him?"

She gave a crooked smile. "About three centuries, give or take a few years."

"I don't need looking after," the sparrow muttered. "Do you think I want you interfering all the time? If you'd just stay away from me, we'd both be happier."

"You know I can't," the minstrel said wearily. "It's been laid on me to look after you."

"You're not allowed to hurt me, either," the sparrow snapped. "You call this not hurting me?"

"I didn't do it," Rookfeather pointed out. "And, anyhow, you're not hurt."

She had made very sure she didn't outright tell Wren what to do, I thought. And she had made certain she did not watch.

"Wait a minute," said Wren. "Three centuries? Three hundred years? How old are you?"

"It's not polite to ask a lady's age," said Rookfeather, with another wry smile. "About three centuries, more or less. He's ten years younger."

"*Laid on you...*" I repeated. "By whom?"

"Our father. After our mother died and we were left alone in the sultan's court. I wanted to leave, but my brother was still so young... My father and I quarreled about it. He wouldn't live among the humans, but he thought my brother needed to stay with our mother's people because he was only a little child, and so I was supposed to stay to look after him. I refused. That was when my father made certain I would have to look after my brother, that I would have to protect him from all harm."

"What are you two talking about?" Wren asked, sounding a little irritated.

"A *geas*," I said. "It's an old, old magic of the Fair Folk. It's a way of..." I scratched my ear and tried to think of the best way to put it. "Of binding someone to do something. Or to not do something. If you lay a *geas* on someone to do something, they have to do it. No matter what. Or, if it's to prevent them doing something, then they absolutely cannot do that thing."

"Or what?" Wren asked.

"They die," I said. "Sometimes. Something very bad happens, anyway. She's saying her father laid a *geas* on her, to protect her brother, to look after him and to do nothing against him. She couldn't stop Abastor taking Liasis, or go and rescue Liasis herself, because that would be going against her brother."

"Oh," said Wren. "So that's why back at Hampstead-Above-The-Falls you couldn't tell us Liasis had been turned into a snake, or exactly where to go to find him, or who had taken him, even though you knew. You tried to say something and couldn't. All you could do was give hints. But I still don't understand. Abastor's not a little child any more. Why hasn't this *geas* thing ended?"

"My father went away," the minstrel said. "And he hasn't come back yet. You know what the Fair Folk are like."

"No," Wren said. "I don't, actually."

"They don't pay much attention to time," I explained. "And actually, time is different in the Fair Folk Mounds, in their underground halls. Her father might come back in another few hundred years and be very surprised to discover they've grown up. But meanwhile…"

"Meanwhile," Rookfeather said, "Abastor Sultanzada…" and although *Sultanzada* is a Callipeplan title, the way she said *Abastor* made me fairly sure that wasn't his real name, any more than Rookfeather was hers. The Fair Folk, like all of us Old Things, have more than one name, and we Old Things don't use our real names lightly. "…Abastor Sultanzada can spend a few years eating thistle-seed and caterpillars."

"He deserves it," said Wren. The sparrow gave her a beady-eyed glower.

I've never believed in letting an important chance slip by.

"I was just telling Wren that she needed to find the right kind of sorcerer to apprentice herself to," I said. "You know, someone who might understand her kind of magic, and the wandering life she wants to live."

"Oh?" said Rookfeather.

"So, are you looking for an apprentice?"

"Did I say I was a sorcerer?" Rookfeather tried to look very surprised.

I gave her a disgusted look. She grinned again, a bit guiltily.

"Apprentices don't like me. I go off wandering for months without telling them and forget to leave them a list of things to do. There's a rookery in the trees outside my tower, and the rooks start cawing at dawn. I hardly ever go to court and, when I do, I usually forget to put on a velvet robe, so they're embarrassed in front of all the other sorcerers because I'm so undignified."

It was Wren's turn to give Rookfeather a disgusted look. "If you can't tell that those are just the sort of things I don't mind, you're not a very good sorcerer. Or a very observant human being."

"Or half-human being," I murmured.

"And I get very bad tempered when I'm working on a new song and it isn't turning out right," Rookfeather added.

"The real question is, are you a good sorcerer or not?" Wren asked.

"Ask Torrie how many sorcerers can turn themselves into birds without a lot of fuss and bother. Or at all, in fact."

"Actually, I meant 'good' as in . . ."

"Ah," said Rookfeather, becoming serious. "That's the important one, of course. I do try to be. I'm not like my brother, I hope."

Wren cleared her throat. "So, um, are you looking for an apprentice?"

"No," said Rookfeather. "But I might offer to teach one, if one showed up. May I see that fancy?"

She took the sparrow fancy from Wren's hand and twirled it in the air. It looked more man-shaped now, and less birdlike.

"Very nice," said Rookfeather, and she tucked it away inside her shirt.

"Er…" said Wren.

"Abastor's tied to it. You don't want it," Rookfeather said firmly. She slid her harp into its sack again and slung it from her shoulder. "I think I *will* teach you, young Wren. For a while. The cows of High Morroway have enough milk-charms for now."

"You were waiting for us, in Hampstead-Above-The-Falls," I said accusingly. "Waiting for Wren."

Rookfeather just smiled. "Come to Callipepla, Wren," she said. "There's a forest of ancient camphor trees in the hills west of the royal city. It belongs to the sultan. In the camphor forest, there's a tower built of red stone."

"And you live there?" Wren asked.

"Once in a while."

"So what do I do if you're not home?" Wren asked.

"Tell the rooks you've arrived," Rookfeather said cheerfully. "Nobody gossips like the crow family." Her smile faded as she looked at the brown sparrow, flicking his tail angrily as he perched on a twig. "I expect I'll be there for the next few years. I'll have to keep an eye on Abastor. Read him books to improve his morals or something boring like that."

"I'd like to see you try," grumbled the sparrow.

Wren squared her shoulders. "All right," she said. "I'll come to Callipepla. For a while."

"A while should be long enough," said Rookfeather. "And we can always go traveling, if we get bored." She gave the sparrow a stern look. "Our cousin umpteen times removed, the sultan, has a very nice aviary for birds in his zoo, and he's always willing to do a favor for a relative." Rookfeather gave me a nod.

"I expect I'll see you again, Torrie."

"You might," I agreed.

The truth was, I was very curious about this sorcerer-minstrel, who was related to both the Fair Folk of the Mounds and the royal family of Callipepla. I made sure I did run into Rookfeather from time to time after that, but it was many, many years—centuries and centuries, to tell the truth—before

Rookfeather ever found her father. And, meanwhile, Abastor had actually... Well, it's quite surprising, what happened to Abastor in the end. But that's a long story, so I won't tell you now.

Rookfeather settled her harp sack more firmly on her shoulder, patted the inner pocket where she had tucked the sparrow-man fancy, and plucked the two glossy black feathers from her hair.

"You can come with me, or not," she told the sparrow. "But it's a very dangerous world for a very small bird, and I have the fancy that can change you back, so you probably should."

The sparrow gave a pathetic cheep, and added glumly, "As if I had any choice. Just remember I *am* a very small bird, and I can't fly as fast as you."

Rookfeather took a feather in each hand, holding them between her thumb and first two fingers. Then she gave a sort of a shrug, and, with a rustle and ripple of all her tattered, colorful silk, she was gone. There was just a shiny black rook, soaring up into the sky. She circled around us once, and cawed.

"Show-off," said the sparrow, and he took off too, in a frantic flapping of feathers.

Wren watched them go with longing in her eyes.

"I'm going to learn to do that," she said firmly, and I knew her thoughts were on the griffin feathers we had found in the mountains. Then she added, "Oh bother! Rookfeather's left me to turn all twenty-seven toads back into Royal Knights."

But actually, she hadn't.

CHAPTER THIRTEEN

In which we return to Castle Morroway

Rookfeather, with the little brown speck that was Abastor following her, was hardly out of sight when we heard Ash whinny and Liasis call, "Wren! Torrie!" from the bottom of the hill.

We started down to meet them. There was actually quite a babble of voices, and it was soon clear why. The prince was leading a troop of twenty-seven knights.

They didn't look very knightly. They were all barefoot, uncombed and unwashed. Their clothes were a strange mixture of odds and ends. Several were wearing only trousers, with towels draped over their shoulders to keep off the sun. A few of the women knights were wearing only tunics, like short dresses down to their knees. A couple of the stouter knights were dressed in nothing but fancy velvet robes, one purple, one black. One was wearing a very ratty old red robe. You can probably guess that while the goblins were looting

Lord Abastor's kitchens, the Royal Knights of Morroway had plundered his wardrobe. From the look of it, there had been barely enough clothes to go around. They were leading Lord Abastor's white mare, too, which I thought was sensible. You never can tell what goblins might decide to eat at a feast.

Liasis introduced us to Sir Acer, the King's Champion—a tall, thin knight with a droopy moustache—as well as his wife, Sir Salix, who was a short, black-haired knight; Sir Eglantine and Sir Rufous, two young knights with copper-bright hair; and the rest. They shook hands with Wren, and even with me.

"I've heard so much about you both," Sir Salix murmured politely, as if we were visiting her at home.

"Well, as much as Liasis had time to explain," said Sir Rufous, grinning. "I want to hear the rest of it as soon as possible."

"I want to hear all of what happened," I said. "I hate only knowing half a story. How did you get your own shapes back?"

"It wasn't me that changed them," said Liasis. "I met them coming across the causeway."

"It was a bird," explained Sir Rufous. "A crow or some-thing."

Sir Salix interrupted to correct him. "A rook."

Sir Rufous shrugged. "Well, it was black and it cawed. It flew in through a crack in the roof and looked at us down in the Pit and said, 'What a bother,' or something like that."

"It wasn't talking like a bird, either," added Sir Eglantine. "It had a human voice. A woman's."

"Well, anyway," Sir Acer took up the story. "It, or she; said, 'Oh, what a bother,' and flew away, down a tunnel, I suppose.

Which we all thought was very strange behavior. And a few moments later she, or it, flew back.

"With a dipper in her claws," said Sir Rufous excitedly.

"A dipper?" I asked.

"Yes, you know, a little pan for dipping up water out of a pail."

"I know what a dipper is," I said. "Why did the rook have a dipper?"

"Just wait and you'll find out," said Liasis, who obviously knew and was enjoying the story.

"And she sort of whirled it as she flew over," said Sir Eglantine, just about as impatient to get to the important part as I was. "And a swirl of water sloshed out…"

"All over us…"

"Cold!"

"And kind of tingly…"

"Fizzy!"

"It was enchanted water," said Sir Salix. "Obviously."

"The crow——"

"Rook! I told you."

"The rook put a spell on it."

"Birds don't do sorcery," said Sir Salix, who obviously should have been one of those teachers who know everything, instead of a knight.

"This one did," said Sir Eglantine.

"Anyway, there we all were," Sir Acer laughed, and his mustache billowed, "suddenly turning back into men and women, twenty-seven of us, jammed into this little pit cut in the rock."

"We just about exploded up out of it."

"Like mushrooms sprouting!" Sir Rufous waved his arms in the air. "Boom!"

"Stark naked!" added Eglantine, giggling.

Sir Salix looked very stern indeed. "We are *not* going to tell the king and queen that part of it. Especially the queen."

"I think you should," said Liasis innocently. "She really doesn't have enough to laugh at in High Morroway."

"The queen does not laugh at the Royal Knights."

"But it might be good for the Royal Knights if she did," said Liasis. "Really, Sir Salix, it doesn't matter. Nobody minds. It happened to me, too. It's *funny*."

Sir Salix didn't look to me like someone who understood funny, but Sir Acer's moustache puffed out again and his eyes twinkled. I could tell that he and King Boiga were going to have a very good laugh at the story of the Twenty-Seven Naked Knights.

"Anyway," he said. "The goblins seemed a bit distracted, so we found what clothing we could, took the horse in case it came in useful, and went to look for the prince."

"And found him," said Sir Eglantine cheerfully.

"I saw you first," said Liasis.

"*I* was looking for a snake."

Liasis held up a hand, ending the teasing argument. "Where's Abastor?" he asked.

Wren and I looked at one another.

"It's a complicated story," she said. "Why don't we put some distance between ourselves and the goblins first, before I tell it. We've got plenty of time, after all; it's a long way to High Morroway."

"And there's really not much for supper," I said gloomily, looking around. "Not for thirty of us."

"Ah," said Sir Rufous. "I did think of that." He patted the white horse, who had a couple of big burlap bags slung over her saddle. "There weren't enough trousers to go around, but I did find a couple of sacks of oatmeal."

"Oh good," I murmured to Wren. "So the goblins are eating plum pudding and ham pies and cheese, and we're eating porridge."

She patted my head in a comforting way. "I have fish-hooks, remember. We can go fishing."

And we did. Although I do have to say, you can get tired of porridge *and* fish very quickly.

WE COLLECTED THE KNIGHTS' HORSES by the dryad's valley, and most of the Knights found their clothes and weapons and armor. This meant that the ones whose garments had been burned up in the fire were able to have more of Abastor's clothes, so we looked a little more respectable as, about a month later, we rode along the well-traveled way to King's Town. It was high summer. The sun was setting, gleaming on the towers of Morroway Castle above us, and on the snowy peaks that were always on the horizon, no matter which direction you looked. Ash's baskets were shared out among the knights' horses so that

Wren could ride, which was why we made better time on our return journey.

"I don't know," she was saying to the prince, as I came back from talking to Sir Eglantine and swung myself up on Abastor's white mare behind Liasis. "I think it must have been your uncle, Prince Notechis."

Wren and Liasis, and the Twenty-Seven Knights, had been arguing about this nearly the whole time since we had left the Great Musquash Swamp: who, in the castle, had been the person helping Lord Abastor? Who had actually thrown the enchanted net over the prince, popped him into a sack, and dropped him over the wall?

Someone—or two someones, Wren and I—had forgotten to ask Lord Abastor this rather important question. Of course, he probably would have enjoyed refusing to answer.

Liasis shook his head. "My uncle would never do anything like that. He just wants a quiet life, fishing."

"Didn't you say that Abastor said it was a woman?"

"It wasn't my stepmother!" Liasis snapped, and Wren looked up, startled, from the scrap of red silk she was carefully attaching to a fancy as she rode. She'd been working on the same one, off and on, since the night she and I captured Thimble. It still had the sprays of heather woven into it, and I still couldn't tell what it was going to be.

"I didn't mean to say it was," she protested.

"Sorry," Liasis mumbled. "It's just that everyone in the villages keeps hinting that it must have been her, and even some of the knights still think that. But Demansia's a good person."

"And Rookfeather is her friend," I pointed out. "It was Queen Demansia who sent Rookfeather to find Wren to rescue you."

"Right," said Liasis. "So it couldn't have been her. And there's no way she'd have helped Lord Abastor. He was doing it all to make trouble for her."

"Who else would want to get rid of you?" Wren asked.

"Don't glare at *me*. I'm not saying the queen *would* want to get rid of you. I'm just asking, who might? Who would gain something with you gone?"

"Or who would gain something from helping Lord Abastor?" I asked. "Those two questions aren't the same, Wren."

Wren frowned. Liasis frowned. I scratched my head. But none of us had any idea.

SOMEONE SAW US COMING, of course. They were keeping a lookout. We had passed through a number of small villages in the past few days, and word had run ahead that the prince was on his way home. By the time we reached the market square in King's Town, nearly the whole population had turned out to line the road, cheering and throwing roses and sunflowers down under our horses' hooves. Some young people had made a bonfire in the middle of the square. People were dancing and singing and passing out toasted cheese on sticks. I wouldn't have minded some toasted cheese about then, but I thought it was probably best if I didn't let the crowd see me.

"Father!" shouted Liasis, and he urged the white mare to a gallop. I squeaked and jumped to Ash's back behind Wren. People scattered out of the prince's way and cheered some more as King Boiga, riding a big chestnut warhorse, came galloping down from the castle. He wasn't alone. Cantering along beside him on a proud gray Callipeplan stallion was Queen Demansia. Behind them came Prince Notechis, and behind him, running and whooping, came all the servants from the castle.

"Son!" roared the king, and the two of them met in a sort of careful crash, if you can imagine that, the two horses jostling and prancing together, the king and prince embracing one another without anybody quite getting a leg crushed.

"Liasis," cried the queen. "Oh, Liasis, you're back!"

Liasis leaned over and flung his arms around her to kiss her cheek. The king tried to hug them both at once and started to tip over, because in his haste he hadn't waited for the groom to cinch his saddle tight enough. They all scrambled down to the ground before there was a nasty accident.

"You saved me, Demansia," Liasis said, quite loudly, standing back and holding the queen's hands. "You sent Rookfeather to find a hero, and she found Wren. That's Wren, on the gray pony," he added. "She's a sorcerer."

The king picked his wife right up off her feet and kissed her, there in front of everyone.

And the people of King's Town cheered. It was a bit ragged and uncertain at first, but Wren stuck two fingers in her mouth and whistled loudly, and pretty soon everyone was calling out the queen's name and cheering for her.

It was the beginning of happier times for Demansia in High Morroway.

"Watch Prince Notechis," whispered Wren in my ear. "Does he look angry?"

"No," I whispered back. "He looks like he's just caught the biggest fish of his life—full of joy. Now he's hugging Liasis. And the king's hugging him."

"So much hugging," sighed Wren. "They look like a really happy family."

"I think that's because they are," I said.

"But someone in the castle betrayed them."

"Hmm," said Sir Eglantine, who, like Wren and I, was watching the castle folk crowding around the king and queen.

"Hmm," I said as well. "I see someone who doesn't look happy."

"Yes," said Wren slowly. "Who's she?"

Sir Eglantine didn't have to ask who we meant. It was obvious. Although the light of the bonfire sparkled on quite a number of teary faces, including that of King Boiga himself, they were all tears of joy. Except for one, a blonde-haired girl in a tidy blue dress and a white apron. She twitched a hasty, nervous smile when the prince hugged her, but it wasn't a real smile. She was shaking so badly she could hardly stand. Fear, I thought. She was terribly, horribly, afraid.

"She's Farancia," Eglantine said quietly. "One of the maids. But we can't accuse her of being in league with a sorcerer and betraying the royal family just because she looks like she's about to throw up."

"Why not?" Wren asked. "Everyone was quick enough to accuse the queen just because she was foreign."

Eglantine looked embarrassed.

Liasis beckoned to us, so Wren slid off Ash and, leaning a bit on her staff, limped up to be introduced to the king and queen. The prince had been telling, with great enthusiasm and much arm-waving, how we had captured Lord Abastor, and as King Boiga shook Wren's hand and Queen Demansia kissed her on both cheeks, he continued.

"And then, wham! Wren swung down and bopped him in the chin and he folded up like he was dead," Liasis said. "We tied him up and when he woke…"

The maid Farancia turned the color of skim milk and fainted.

I was the first one to get to her, and Eglantine was next. Eglantine stood there, looking a bit grim, her hand on the hilt of her sword, while I rubbed Farancia's wrists and fanned her face. Her eyes fluttered open again and she sat up. I let her see me, and the king and queen too.

"Erk!" the maid said, staring at me, and then she burst into tears and tried to crawl away.

Sir Eglantine caught her arms and pulled her to her feet, supporting her while everyone stared in astonishment.

"Farancia?" asked Liasis. "What's wrong? Don't be afraid of Torrie, he's the Old Thing of the Wild Forest, not a goblin. He's really very nice when you get to know him…"

"I didn't mean to, I didn't want to!" Farancia cried, her words choked by the great gulping sobs breaking out of her. "I had to do it, I had to."

"What did you have to do?" Sir Eglantine asked grimly.

"Why did you have to do it?" Wren asked, more kindly.

"He said he could cure my mother—and he did, he gave me a potion, it had magic in it, he said it could make her better, and it did, it did. I had to do what I promised, I had to put that charm on the prince to change him and give him to Abastor, I didn't want to but I had to, so that he'd give me the rest of the medicine."

I really hoped Rookfeather kept Abastor as a sparrow for a long, long time.

Everyone stared in horror and that sort of embarrassment you feel when someone else has done something wrong and shameful.

"Oh, Farancia," said the queen. "Oh, my dear."

"Was your mother cured?" Wren asked.

Farancia sniffed and wiped her face with her apron, but sobs still kept breaking out, like hiccoughs. "Her heart's much stronger. Her lips don't go all blue whenever she gets out of bed. She can even dig in her garden now, and that's always been what she liked best. But…but…oh, Your Highness, Your Highness!" She tore free of Eglantine's grasp and flung herself down at Liasis's feet, clasping him around the knees. "I'm so sorry! I'm so very, very sorry!"

Liasis put his hand gently on her head.

King Boiga sighed. "Take her to the castle," he said quietly to Sir Eglantine and Sir Rufous, who were the closest knights. Then he leaned over and kissed his wife once more, tightened the girth of his horse's saddle, and climbed back on. "Roast beef!" he shouted, over the whole square. "Wine! Fireworks! Music! My son—our son—has been rescued! I declare tonight a festival!"

So all of King's Town feasted and sang and danced by the light of the blazing bonfire.

Several weeks passed. Word spread quickly throughout all of High Morroway that the prince had been rescued and that a sorcerer, an enemy of the queen, was to blame. Word also spread of the queen's obvious love for the prince, and how she had sent Wren the Sorcerer (that wasn't how it happened, but it's what people said) to rescue him. Suddenly, people couldn't praise the queen enough. They said they'd known all along she had nothing to do with it.

Well, that's humans for you.

No one was sure what to do with the maid, Farancia. She should have been tried for treason, but Liasis didn't want that. However, what she had done was very wrong. Doing it to save someone else did not make it right. Liasis and the Knights could so easily have been killed, or trapped forever in the Forest, or turned into animals for good. Eventually the king and his councillors decided to send the maid into exile. She was to leave High Morroway and not come back for seven years.

"You're more merciful than I deserve, Your Grace," Farancia whispered when she was told. And, as it turned out, she went down to Erythroth. Her mother joined her and they made a new start there, where nobody knew or cared what Farancia had done. But they never came back to High Morroway.

Liasis and Prince Notechis and I went fishing. He really was a very nice man, who just wanted a quiet life. Wren spent a lot of time in the library studying maps of the lands between High Morroway and Callipepla.

King Boiga and Queen Demansia told Wren that once she had finished her apprenticeship, she was welcome to come back to High Morroway to be their Court Sorcerer, although, being a poor kingdom, they wouldn't be able to provide her with very many velvet robes. (That was actually Liasis's joke, not mine.) But Wren said she didn't think she'd ever want to settle down as Court Sorcerer anywhere, at which the prince looked rather disappointed.

"Perhaps," the queen said, "you could be an Official Visiting Sorcerer."

"I'd like that," Wren said. "But I'm a long way from being a real sorcerer yet."

FINALLY, the day arrived that Wren had set for her departure. Autumn had come, cool and crisp, and the Royal Cheese Fair was only a week away. The Royal Family gave her all sorts of practical things for her long journey south, like new boots and clothes, and money, and more personal gifts too. Liasis gave her a kit of knives and pliers and coils of interesting wires for making fancies, and the queen shyly gave her a silk caftan (like a long gown with a sash), for wearing on hot summer days in Callipepla, along with a letter to take to Rookfeather. The king gave her a fine new saddle and bridle for Ash, since he wasn't a pedlar's pony covered in baskets anymore, and Eglantine gave her a book to write spells in, once she learned some. I gave her a nice collection of interesting feathers I had gathered in the woods around the castle, although none of them were as interesting as griffin feathers.

Liasis and I rode along with Wren for the first few miles. Then, by the side of a chortling mountain stream, we had a picnic, for old times' sake.

Afterwards, Liasis packed up the remains of a very nice lunch of fish and cheese pie and Wren leaned against a rock, tying a last few knots in the ribbons of that fancy with the sprigs of heather in it. The wind gusted around us, sending a flurry of yellow birch leaves dancing.

"Well," said Wren, holding the fancy up into the air and watching it dance, too. "That's that." We watched the fancy twist in the air, first with sudden, darting movements, and then slow, stately turns.

"It's a bird?" Liasis guessed.

"It's a wren," Wren said, and she blushed a little. "At least, it's meant to be. But sometimes it seems to look more like…" She thrust it at me. "Here. It's for you, Torrie. I'm not sure if it's quite finished."

"Some things are never meant to be entirely finished," I said, taking it and studying it. "It's an eagle," I added.

Wren shrugged, but I could tell she was pleased. She took something else out of her pocket. "And this one's for you, Liasis."

"Beautiful!" said the prince.

It was the shining sky-dragon she had been making the evening I met her.

Wren smiled, with the quiet pride that comes from knowing you've made something well, and that people love it.

"I guess it's time to go," she said, and whistled for Ash.

"But you're going to come back," Liasis said firmly.

"Of course. I'll come see you whenever I'm in High Morroway."

"It'll be a much shorter trip once you learn to fly."

"If I learn to fly."

"You will. You can do anything."

Wren laughed. "But Ash would be so disappointed to be left behind. It's a long journey, but we'll have to come to High Morroway the usual way."

"I suppose." Liasis sighed. "Well, we can't stay here all day." He looked at Wren and me. "I guess I should be getting back. We're going fishing with my uncle this evening, right, Torrie?"

"Right."

He and Wren shook hands before he mounted and rode back up the road. It was nice of Liasis to see that Wren and I wanted to say our farewells in private.

"So," said Wren.

"So," I said.

"I'm off."

"You are."

"To Callipepla."

"Yes."

"Come with me, Torrie."

I shook my head. "Not yet. I need to pay more attention to the Wild Forest, I think. For a little while. And I should keep an eye on what Bobbin and her goblins are getting up to in the Great Musquash."

Wren nodded, understanding this. "But you will come see me in Callipepla, some time?"

"Oh yes," I said. "I want to see the camphor forest." I hesitated. "Wren?"

"Yes?"

"I know you want to keep traveling and seeing new things. But a home isn't a cage, you know, when it's *your* home. And even wandering sorcerers need a place to keep their books and whatnot. So if someday you find you want to build a tower of your own…well, there's always those ruins by the Great Musquash. It might be nice to rebuild that old tower, someday."

Wren laughed. "I don't know about the neighbors, though."

I waved a hand. "Goblins get bored easily. They're bound to move back to the mountains before too long."

"All right," said Wren. "Someday."

We looked at one another. Then Wren laughed again. "If you haven't come to visit me in a year or two, Torrie, I'll figure out a way to turn into a griffin, and I'll come and get you myself."

And she swung up into the saddle and rode off, trying very hard not to look back.

"Look after her!" I called to Ash.

He gave a horsy laugh and flicked his tail. "You know she's perfectly capable of looking after herself, Torrie. But I will."

I headed back up the road towards King's Town. I found the white mountain horse waiting patiently by a high shoulder of rock. The prince was standing atop the outcrop of stone like a sentry on a tower, so I scrambled up to join him.

From there, we could watch Wren riding down the steep and winding road until she dwindled to a tiny distant figure on a shadow-gray pony.

Just before she rode out of sight behind a stand of dark pines, she turned and looked back, knowing we'd be there. She waved her old hat cheerfully in the air.

And then she was gone.

OF COURSE, when I did go down to Callipepla and the camphor forest, I found Wren in the middle of a very interesting adventure of her own, and, much later, bits of it even got mixed up with my dragon-slaying quest. But the sun's coming up and that's a story for another time.

In case you missed the first two Torrie adventures, be sure to read

Torrie & the Pirate-Queen

Torrie, the Old Thing from the Wild Forest, helps Anna and her ragtag crew of retired pirates on a dramatic quest to rescue Anna's captive father.

Torrie & the Firebird

Torrie joins Anna on an adventurous quest to recover a stolen gem and prove the innocence of Kokako, a young boy fleeing an angry mob.

About the author & the illustrator

K.V. Johansen is the author of six novels for young people, a history of children's books, and a series of picture books. She lives in Sackville, New Brunswick.

Christine Delezenne is the illustrator of several books for young people. She lives in Montréal, Québec